BOOK FOU

CAN ANY POWER ON EARTH SAVE VICTORIA WINTERS
FROM THE SUPERNATURAL MENACE OF THE PHANTOM
MARINER?

*According to legend, death at Collinwood is preceded by an eerie
warning: a black-robed figure with a skull instead of a face appears to
the victim. The appearance of this Phantom Mariner is an irrevocable
death sentence.*

*When Victoria sees the phantom, she refuses to believe it is real. She
tries to tell herself it is someone playing a macabre trick – perhaps the
beautiful Linda, who intends to marry the man Victoria loves; perhaps
Linda's sinister father, a gifted hypnotist who seems to be willing
Victoria to her grave. Victoria is willing to suspect anyone.*

*FOR IF HUMAN HANDS ARE NOT BEHIND THE GHOST, THEN
VICTORIA MUST SURELY DIE...*

Hermes Press

Originally published 1967

Published by Hermes Press, an imprint of
Herman and Geer Communications, Inc.

Daniel Herman, Publisher
Troy Musguire, Production Manager
Eileen Sabrina Herman, Managing Editor
Alissa Fisher, Graphic Design
Kandice Hartner, Senior Editor
Benjamin Beers, Archivist

2100 Wilmington Road
Neshannock, Pennsylvania 16105
(724) 652-0511
www.HermesPress.com; info@hermespress.com

Book design by Eileen Sabrina Herman
First printing, 2020

LCCN applied for: 10 9 8 7 6 5 4 3 2 1 0
ISBN 978-1-61345-198-4
OCR and text editing by H + G Media and Eileen Sabrina Herman
Proof reading by Eileen Sabrina Herman and Fey Wagner

From Dan, Louise, Sabrina, Jacob, Ruk'us and Noodle for D'zur and Mellow

*Acknowledgments: This book would not be possible without the help and
encouragement of Jim Pierson and Curtis Holdings*

Printed in Canada

THE MYSTERY
OF COLLINWOOD
by Marilyn Ross

CONTENTS

CHAPTER 1 6

CHAPTER 2 18

CHAPTER 3 30

CHAPTER 4 42

CHAPTER 5 54

CHAPTER 6 66

CHAPTER 7 77

CHAPTER 8 88

CHAPTER 9 100

CHAPTER 10 111

CHAPTER 11 122

CHAPTER 12 133

CHAPTER 1

Victoria Winters stood before the big living-room window of Collinwood with its wide view of Widow's Hill and the Atlantic beyond. Her sensitive, pretty face wore a look of fear as she drew a hand through the silky black hair that tumbled about her shoulders. Never in all her young life had she witnessed nature in such ferocity and never before had she been so thoroughly terrified by its unrelenting violence beyond any control!

The stately old mansion, which Jeremiah Collins had built to withstand the cruel seasons of the Maine coast year after year, century after century, even, enduring such storms of hurricane force as this it was now experiencing, was creaking and groaning like a fine old schooner battling for its existence in savage seas. And in a sense it was exactly what the old house was doing.

The storm had been preceded by an eerie calm that had lasted for forty-eight hours. The weather had been strangely warm for the coastal town at this time in late September. Weird varieties of insects accompanied the uncomfortable humidity and a lazy haze seemed to encompass both the land and the ocean beyond. At the same time radio and television stations issued regular ominous warnings that the storm was playing havoc along the Florida coastline and in the southern regions. The days, and then the hours, before its impact might be felt in that part of northeast Maine had been solemnly announced. And yet for the most part no one had believed an early storm of such proportions possible.

A few precautions had been taken. Roger Collins had ordered in the fishing fleet that kept the Collins Packing Company supplied and directed that the ships in the harbor be securely tied. Elizabeth Stoddard, his sister, the mistress of Collinwood as well as president of the cannery which supplied the family wealth, had made a careful check of the outbuildings and of the house itself, keeping Matt Morgan, the handyman and sole servant at the mansion, busy with hasty repairs of roofs, windows and shutters which he hadn't nearly completed when the hurricane broke.

Only minutes ago a shutter on a second-floor window had wrenched partly free, crashing through the glass. Elizabeth and the handyman were upstairs now coping with the damage and securing the window against the wind and torrential rains. Long ago the electricity had failed and, shortly afterward, the telephone line. The last call had come from Roger Collins, who had decided to remain in his office at the cannery.

"All hell has broken loose along the shore," had been his brusque comment over the already crackling wires. "The waves must be a foot high over the wharf and every time the wind strikes they're washing against my windows."

Roger Collins' office was on the second floor of the shore-located factory, which gave them some idea of the fury of the hurricane. A query brought the information that in spite of precautions one of the fishing fleet was missing and several pleasure boats out from Portland had been caught, and presumably lost, in the storm. A couple of coast guard patrol ships were braving the seas to try to reach them and a Liberian freighter that had wired she was in trouble and taking water fast.

The storm had come to full fury several hours ago. While it had changed course somewhat, making it less deadly, the weather office offered no hope of it lessening until early evening. By that time it was supposed to dissipate in a tropical downpour that would last until dawn. Elizabeth's teen-age daughter, Carolyn, had left a battery-operated transistor radio behind when she'd gone to Ellsworth to finish her final year in high school there, and it was their only contact with the outside world at this moment.

As Victoria watched the sea with frightened eyes she held the small radio in her hand. The announcer from the Bangor station was offering a continuous, excited commentary on the progress of the storm. "The eye of the hurricane seems to have reached this district," he was saying. "We are operating on our emergency power plant, as all electric power is off in this area. Many phone lines are down and the streets are dangerous because of falling objects. A large sign has just toppled off the shopping market building and there are wires down and other risks. The roads are equally hazardous and we urge you to remain in the comparative safety of your homes!"

Victoria found herself wondering just how safe even a large building like Collinwood might be? The sprawling mansion of forty-odd rooms was located in such an exposed position on this cliff overlooking the sea that it was getting the brunt of the hurricane.

The great elm trees decorating the grounds bent so sharply before the rage of the gale that she feared some of them would come crashing down. The normally calm ocean was terrifying. The waves seemed mountainous and the frothy white caps were everywhere. Perhaps the lash of the rain and the moaning and screaming of the winds were the most frightening. Although Victoria had been at Collinwood for more than a year, she had never witnessed such a storm before.

Turning away from the window, she stood surveying the murky room. It was almost as dark as late evening. Her eyes touched briefly on the portraits of those long-ago members of the Collins family who had lived in the old house. Had any of them witnessed a storm like this?

As if in reply to her unspoken question the radio announcer stated, "This is the worst hurricane to hit the Maine coast since the late nineteen-thirties. In October of 1939 a storm of even more terrifying force left devastation and a toll of lost lives we hope will not be matched today!"

With a frown crossing her attractive, sensitive face, she turned off the radio with its continuous recital of danger and doom. It seemed to her she might be better off without it for a while. She wondered how Elizabeth and Matt were making out with the damage upstairs.

Moving down the long room to stand before the big brick fireplace she wondered how David was doing in the storm. The boy, Roger Collins' little son, had been her reason for coming to this isolated old mansion by the sea —the boy, and her own desire to trace her origins and discover if she was actually a member of the Collins family herself.

Elizabeth's letter had arrived at the foundling home where she'd been raised from infancy and to which she had returned as a teacher. The letter had out of the blue and mysteriously offered her the post of governess to the difficult young David. And because Collinsport was fairly close to Bangor and was linked in her mind with a monthly check that arrived at the foundling home for her from Bangor for many years, she decided to take the position.

The hurricane increased in fury momentarily and the wind in the chimney took on a new shrill note of frenzied shrieking—cold mocking sound, as if to express the frustration she had known in her long months at the old house. She had not been able to find out anything about herself that counted. She was sure there was some connection between herself and the Collins family and that was why Elizabeth had wanted her there. But she had not been able to hit on any solid proof.

The mystery man of the village, the returned millionaire Burke Devlin, had taken pity on her plight and been sympathetic toward her. But even he had discouraged her hope of finding the secret to her ancestry. Still, she had remained and in the process had found romance with Ernest Collins, the talented violinist cousin of Elizabeth and Roger. Ernest was in Europe now, far from this storm, but he had written her that he would be arriving in Maine on vacation in a few weeks and she had been eagerly awaiting his appearance. Long ago he had professed his love for her and there was no doubt in her heart that she truly loved him. She hoped on this visit he might offer her a ring and set a date for their marriage. But whether he was ready for this or not—the tragedy of his unhappy first marriage still seemed to haunt him at times—she would be glad to see him.

Perhaps her romance with Ernest had been the only truly pleasant experience in this house of dark shadows and many secrets. From the beginning Roger Collins had been difficult. Elizabeth's weakly handsome younger brother had at first tried to flirt with her. When she would have none of that, and turned to Ernest instead, Roger had become sour and critical of her handling of his son's tutoring.

His tendency to drink too much had not made it any easier, either. It had been in one of his sullen, drunken moods that he'd decided he would send the youngster to the boarding school in Augusta he himself had attended and that was where David was at this moment.

Victoria turned to stare out the window from the distant point of the fireplace. Even this far away, the angry storm was a frightening spectacle. Perhaps it would not be so bad in Augusta, which was further inland. But surely Ellsworth would be getting the full force of the hurricane, and that was where Carolyn, Elizabeth's daughter, a pleasant girl near her own age, was boarding and attending high school.

Victoria missed Carolyn; they'd had many pleasant times together. Elizabeth had insisted Victoria remain in the big house as her companion. But the older woman, though kindly in nature, was often remote and strange. Shattered by the disappearance of her husband nearly twenty years earlier, she had remained a prisoner of the old mansion ever since. Not once in all the intervening years had she ventured outside its doors. There were many sinister speculations in the village as to why she reacted to her loss in this way. Some gossips even hinted that Elizabeth might have had a hand in murdering her missing mate. But Victoria refused to listen to such wild accusations and continued to firmly believe the attractive, dignified woman had merely taken this way of showing her heartbreak.

At Collinwood one soon learned not to ask too many questions. Much had to be accepted for what it was. Victoria prided herself that in spite of initial difficulties she had managed to stay on and gradually be accepted as one of them.

From somewhere outside there came a crash as something gave way before the hurricane to strike with shattering impact against the house. She thought of the cottage a short distance away, which Elizabeth had rented again only a few weeks ago. After it had remained vacant most of the summer, a tenant had suddenly arrived for it.

A strange, sad tenant, in Victoria's opinion. Margaret Lucas, the middle-aged woman who had come to live in the cottage for a while, had explained she was there to recuperate from a serious operation. She made it plain she wanted privacy and quiet. Victoria and Elizabeth guessed she might be a terminal cancer case who had been given only a short period to live and who had decided to spend her last days in isolation from friends and relatives. Her wan, pale face and emaciated body helped to suggest this. Her iron-gray hair was heavy, and she invariably wore dark glasses.

She had only a single companion with her, a male servant who looked after her household duties, cooked the meals and drove her tiny foreign car. He was even stranger than his mistress, a dark, menacing-looking hunchback of southern European extraction, whose name was Carlos Marelli. His gargoyle features, together with his heavy lips and dark hair low on a receding forehead, made an ugly combination. But except for being tight-lipped and surly, he was not too difficult. He went quietly about his duties and was obviously very devoted to his mistress.

Victoria liked Margaret Lucas and the new tenant of the cottage seemed to take to her. She was the only one Margaret Lucas welcomed to her place. Victoria found the invalid easy to talk to and before she realized it had begun to use her as a confidante. She had even spoken frankly to the Lucas woman of her love for Ernest and her hopes that they might soon have a future together. Margaret Lucas, in turn, had been an interested listener and expressed curiosity about Ernest. She had asked Victoria to be sure and bring him to meet her when he came. As the storm raged on, Victoria hoped that it might not be so noticeable in the smaller cottage.

Lost in these thoughts, she started abruptly when suddenly the front door bell rang with a jangling shrillness. She couldn't imagine who would be at the door on such an afternoon. The urgent summons of the bell came impatiently once again. With a puzzled frown on her pretty face, Victoria hurried the length of the big living room to see who it was.

The somber shadows of the hallway made her hesitate before the door. Outside, the hurricane still raged; and certainly no one was expected. Carefully she turned the heavy brass handle and swung the great oak door open. The rush of wind and rain made her step back quickly. The door swung wider than she had intended.

And now there stood revealed in the doorway a figure as strange as any she had ever seen. Facing her in the uncertain light was a tall, gaunt-faced man dressed entirely in black. His long raincape was blowing wildly in the storm and his hand was pressed protectively against the wide brim of his foreign-style black hat. Her immediate thought, because of the eerie light, the storm and his dress, was that this was the devil himself.

He stepped inside, the rain dripping down his bony, sallow face, his sunken, bright eyes fixed on her appraisingly. "I do not believe we have met," he said in a pleasant voice pitched above the storm. "I am Professor Mark Veno. Mrs. Stoddard is expecting my daughter and myself for a visit. We have had the misfortune to arrive in this storm."

Victoria had heard nothing about this, but then, it was a house of surprises. So she said, "I'm sure if Mrs. Stoddard is expecting you she'll be glad to know you're here safely."

"We were not to arrive until the weekend, but we made a change in schedule and managed to get here earlier," Professor Veno said. "I will get my daughter and have the driver of the cab bring in our luggage." And with that he swept out into the storm once more. Victoria closed the door slightly against the wind and rain and waited for him to come back.

He returned in a moment with a slim, dark-haired girl on his arm. She was wearing a blue trench coat and a hat of the same material against the storm. The first thing about her that struck Victoria was that the girl to a surprising degree resembled herself! Professor Veno's daughter had the same coloring and features almost identical to her own.

Ben Woodson, one of the two Collinsport cabdrivers, came in after them laden with luggage, a piece in each hand and another under each arm. He plunked them down by Victoria with a grin. "Best kind of ballast for a day like this," he said.

"I wonder that you were able to find your way out here," she said, closing the door.

Ben removed his dripping hat and shook it over the tile of the hallway. "Except for a tree I had to get out and shove back, the road through the woods wasn't too bad."

To Professor Veno, he added, "That will be three dollars, mister."

The man in the raincape was already digging in his trousers pocket. He produced a roll of bills and drew one from it. "Here's five, keep the change. And a safe journey back!"

Ben took the money with a grin. "Thanks! There aren't any kinds of weather I don't drive in," he informed them all. "Blizzard, hurricane or ninety-degree-heat! It's all the same to me." He put on his cap again and Victoria opened the door for him.

When she had closed it carefully after him, against the still-furious winds and rain, she said, "I'll tell Mrs. Stoddard you're here. She's upstairs overseeing the repair of a window the storm broke open."

"There is no hurry," Professor Veno assured her suavely. He had removed his wide-brimmed black hat and she saw that he was almost bald except for a few strands of dark hair plastered across the dome of his head.

"Such an awful day! Have you been here before?" Victoria asked.

His bony face took on a mocking smile. "Indeed, I have. Before I began my world travels I lived in this region. And I have returned many times as a guest of Mrs. Stoddard. And so has my daughter. Allow me to introduce her. My daughter, Linda!"

"Welcome to our storm-tossed house!" Victoria said with a rueful smile.

"Thank you," the dark girl replied. And Victoria noticed she spoke with the barest suggestion of an accent.

Professor Mark Veno took off his raincape. "I believe you must be new to the house?"

"Yes, in a sense," she said. "I've been here a little over a year. I came as governess to David Collins and have remained as a companion to Mrs. Stoddard."

"Ah, yes." The gaunt face showed interest. "You are the Victoria Winters she wrote me about." His daughter regarded her in a cool, arrogant fashion, and Victoria couldn't help wondering if Linda had also noticed their strange resemblance to one another.

At this moment Elizabeth Stoddard came down the stairs with Matt Morgan behind her. The instant she saw Mark Veno and his daughter her face took on an incredulous smile.

"Don't tell me you two managed to get here in spite of the storm!" she said, coming down to throw her arms around the aloof Linda. "I didn't expect either of you until Saturday," she said, kissing the girl on the cheek.

For the first time Linda smiled. "Daddy was able to leave sooner than he'd expected."

"How nice!" Elizabeth said, turning to the somberly dressed professor. "It's unfortunate the weather is so awful. You've met Victoria?"

"She let us in," the professor agreed. "We left most our baggage in New York. But we should have enough in these four bags to take care of our stay here."

Elizabeth turned to Matt Morgan, who had been standing in the background with a grimly knowing expression on his broad, tanned face. "Matt, will you take these bags upstairs? The professor and his daughter will be having the bedrooms just over the hallway here on the second floor. The professor will take the large room."

Matt merely nodded and went forward to gather up the bags in the same fashion in which the cabdriver had managed them. It seemed to Victoria a heavy load, but then, he would have to make only one trip upstairs with them, carrying them that way.

As Matt slowly left them with his heavy burden, the professor called out, "The blue bags are mine and the white ones should be left in my daughter's room."

There was something about the professor's familiarity with Collinwood that Victoria found odd. He behaved as if he had a complete knowledge of the big mansion and its inhabitants, yet he was apparently only a casual guest who had been there a few times before.

His raincape folded over his arm, the professor smiled at Elizabeth Stoddard. "You are looking as young and attractive as ever, Elizabeth."

Elizabeth, neatly pretty in a blue and green afternoon dress, seemed to enjoy the compliment. "Thank you," she said. "I'm afraid I'm aging like everyone else." And she swung around to Linda. "But Linda is growing up into a marvelous beauty."

"Her looks are the chief attraction of our entertainment," the professor said.

Observing Victoria's mild expression of surprise, Elizabeth smiled and explained, "I think I should tell you about the professor and Linda. They perform one of the most complicated mind-reading and mentalism acts in the world. They have starred in all the big European theatres and night clubs."

Professor Veno bowed Victoria's way and with a mocking smile, said, "Not to mention our dates in this country in New York, Las Vegas and Florida. We are leaving for Europe again and an extended tour when we end our stay here."

Linda, who had unbuttoned her raincoat and taken off the

blue hat, spoke up with an eager smile that animated her sensitive face. "And we saw Ernest in Spain. At almost the same time we met last year."

Elizabeth raised her eyebrows with delicate interest. "Really?"

"He was looking very well," Linda went on. "And he said something about coming here for a visit shortly."

"We are expecting him," Elizabeth agreed with a small smile for Victoria. "It is likely you'll all meet here."

Mark Veno appeared pleased with this news. He nodded knowingly. "Linda and Ernest have become very close friends. I'm sure she won't be disappointed if he turns up."

"Daddy!" the girl protested and Victoria noticed she was suddenly blushing.

Elizabeth sighed. "We have no electricity or phone, but there are candles and a few lamps available. And we still have lots of hot water in the tank if you feel like having showers. Luckily, we do a great deal of our cooking on a wood stove in the kitchen so I can promise you some food."

Linda said, "Please don't worry about us! Just so long as we're safely inside." She hesitated as the wind howled again. "When do they expect the storm to end?"

"The last word was that the hurricane would ease by dusk and the rain that follows it will end about dawn," Victoria volunteered.

"I'm sure the worst must be over now," Elizabeth told her guests. "Why don't you go up and unpack and make yourselves comfortable? Victoria and I will have dinner ready for you early."

"There is no need to rush," Mark Veno assured her. "We had a good lunch on the train coming down." He directed his sunken, keen eyes Victoria's way. "I've looked forward to meeting you, Miss Winters. Elizabeth's letters aroused my deep interest in you. We must have a good talk." And then to his daughter, "Come, Linda." Linda gave her a brief appraising glance before she joined her father and started upstairs.

Elizabeth and Victoria were left alone in the shadowed hallway as the other two vanished upstairs. Victoria thought Veno a most mysterious, almost sinister figure and was astonished at the way her employer had so readily accepted him into the house. She had also been startled and disturbed to hear his daughter speak with so much warmth of Ernest.

Elizabeth listened to the rain and wind a moment and then with a tiny shudder said, "It doesn't sound much better. Let's go out to the kitchen and see how things are there."

The storm did not seem as bad in the rear of the house and Victoria at once started a fire in the big wood stove. As soon as the paper between the logs began to blaze she quickly put down the lid and turned to her employer.

"Professor Veno and his daughter are very unusual," she said.

Elizabeth was tying on an apron. "I agree," she said. "They are originals. The professor is really very famous in his way. After losing his wife, he trained his daughter to take her place with him in his act as soon as she was old enough. She's only nineteen now." Elizabeth gave her a sharp glance. "You two look something alike. You should be pleased. She's turned into a beauty."

"They both strike me as being brilliant," Victoria said, dodging the subject.

"Yes. Besides being an outstanding mentalist, the professor has also taken a great interest in the spirit world. He has written and sold a great many articles on ghost lore in various sections of the globe. He did a piece about our own Widow's Hill."

"That is interesting," Victoria agreed. "And they spoke of meeting Ernest."

"They wrote about that," Elizabeth said, looking somewhat embarrassed. "I don't think there is anything like a serious friendship between Ernest and the girl. It's only natural they valued meeting him when they were all so far away from home."

"Yes, I suppose so," Victoria agreed quietly. But she was more than a little concerned. Linda's manner suggested that she had a genuine crush on the violinist. Had Ernest encouraged her attention?

By the time they had dinner under way, the hurricane had declined slightly in its force. Dusk had settled very early, so at Elizabeth's bidding Victoria had placed two large candelabra on the dining room table and lit the half-dozen big white candles to give her light while she set the table.

Roger Collins returned from the cannery in time to join them at dinner and when Elizabeth told him about their guests he looked a good deal less than pleased.

"What is he doing back here again?" the blond man demanded. "And what possessed him to come on a wild day like this?"

Elizabeth, helping Victoria set out the silver, took it quietly, looking the charming hostess in a long crimson gown that was enhanced by the soft glow of the candles. She glanced up at the irritated face of her brother and said calmly, "The professor can come here whenever he likes. You know you shouldn't make all this fuss. And do try to be civil to him. At least for Linda's sake."

"Damned pretty girl!" Roger muttered. "If it weren't for her I'd show him the door, storm or no storm!"

No more was said. And when they were all finally seated around the table with its gleaming white cloth and sparkling silver, the dinner had the air of a festive occasion. In the flattering glow of the candles, Victoria felt that dining rooms, at least, had no need for electricity.

All through the excellent steak dinner, Professor Veno kept up a continuous offering of interesting talk. Roger Collins looked annoyed, but gave a good deal of smiling attention to the pretty Linda who had donned a yellow gown with orange trimming for the occasion. Victoria, in a plain dark dress, felt drab. The storm had eased, but the wind and rain still whipped about the old mansion.

It was after an especially heavy lash of rain on the windows of the dining room that Professor Veno's bony face took on a smile. "Such a night makes me think of the Phantom Mariner."

Roger turned angrily from talking to Linda. "We can do without your ghost stories, Professor!"

The sunken eyes of the black-garbed man at the foot of the table showed a gleam of ironic humor. "I know how you feel about such things, Roger," he said. "But I thought the legend might be of interest to Victoria."

Elizabeth spoke placatingly from the head of the table. "The professor published an essay on our local ghost in *Yankee* magazine."

"Really?" Victoria said. "I don't believe I've heard about it."

Mark Veno nodded. "I thought you mightn't have," he agreed. "I'll make it brief. As you know, this spot where the house was built by Jeremiah Collins is known as Widow's Hill because it was here fishermen's wives came to gather after any bad storm for a first sight of the returning vessels. And it was here they usually learned whether husband, father or son was safe—or lost. The legend has it that whenever there was a death an eerie figure appeared before the wife, sweetheart or mother and stared into her face. Once the woman had come to meet the Phantom Mariner there was no cause for hope."

Victoria was startled by the account. "What sort of figure was this phantom?"

The sunken eyes met hers as the professor went on in his almost hypnotic voice, "Legend has it the figure the weeping women encountered wore a sweeping black cloak and cowl that made him invisible to all but the bereft woman. But when the cowl was opened the features of the Phantom Mariner were those of a skeleton—the face of death itself."

"And it has truly become a legend?" Victoria said.

The flickering light of the candles reflected on the professor's bony white face, giving it for a moment the appearance of a grinning skull's head. "Yes," he said in his strange, soft voice. "To this day the locals believe that to meet the Phantom Mariner face to face is to have a warning of their own death or that of someone dear to them."

"Rot!" Roger Collins said violently, his face flushed from

anger and too many cocktails before dinner. "I'm a local and I don't believe it!"

"You are perhaps merely the exception," the professor said softly.

Elizabeth quickly changed the talk to a comparison of the present hurricane with the one that had swept up the coast in 1939 and wiped away whole wharves, doing untold damage to shipping and taking many lives.

"The death toll won't be so big this time, since we had lots of warning," was Roger's prediction. "But the damage will be even greater than before."

As soon as dinner was over, Elizabeth and Victoria were left to clear away while the others gathered in the living room. Elizabeth took Victoria aside and said, "The storm has eased. I wish you'd go over to the cottage and see if Mrs. Lucas is all right. I don't want her to think we've forgotten her."

Victoria quickly put on her raincoat, high boots and a plastic kerchief. Braving the storm, she walked along the path by the outbuildings that led to the cottage. The wind made her brace herself forward and the rain ran down her face. Ahead she saw the dim glow of an oil lamp in one of the cottage windows.

When she finally reached the cottage and rapped on the door it was the sullen hunchback, Carlos, who answered it. He regarded her suspiciously. "Yes?"

Victoria inquired how they had made out in the storm. "We were worried," she explained, almost apologetically.

"Everything is all right," Carlos said curtly. "Mrs. Lucas has a headache and has retired."

"Tell her I was here and I'll be back in the morning," Victoria said. And she left the cottage to return through the stormy darkness.

She hadn't gone more than a quarter way long the path when she saw a movement in the shadows ahead. She halted, sudden panic rising up in her. And then from the stormy darkness emerged a weird apparition. And for just an instant she got a glimpse of the shadowy figure's face. It wasn't a face, but a grinning skull! She screamed in terror, remembering the legend of the Phantom Mariner.

CHAPTER 2

At the moment she screamed, the grinning skull face blacked out. As she stared wide-eyed into the rainy darkness, the weird figure gradually melted away. Victoria stood there numbed by the experience and almost convinced she had seen an actual ghost. A sharp gust of wind brought the cool rain slashing against her and roused her from her trance-like state.

And then she began to race towards the house. Head bent against the storm, she lurched along the path, stumbling and gasping for breath, but not slowing down for an instant until she touched the handle of the rear door and let herself inside.

Elizabeth was just coming out to the kitchen again. "You look as if you'd seen a ghost!" she said. "What is wrong?"

Victoria pushed back the kerchief from her head and began opening her coat. "Nothing really," she said, still short of breath, and loath to tell Elizabeth Stoddard what she thought she had seen. "I guess there was too much ghost talk at the dinner table. My nerves got the better of me on the way back and I began running from all the phantoms of the night."

Elizabeth's attractive face showed sympathy. "I shouldn't have sent you on that errand alone," she said. "I should have had Matt Morgan or Roger go over there. But Mrs. Lucas gets so upset if strangers visit her and she likes you."

"It was all right," Victoria said, gradually recovering herself and slipping off her coat. "I saw Carlos and he told me there had been no storm damage, but Mrs. Lucas had gone to bed early."

"Just so long as everything is all right over there," Elizabeth said. "Would you like to go in and keep Linda company in the living room for a while? She's all alone. Both Roger and her father went up to their rooms almost as soon as you left."

The words had a special meaning for Victoria. If Professor Veno had gone upstairs so early, he would have had plenty of time to don a disguise and come out and meet her along the path to terrify her. But why?

From the time she'd first encountered the mysterious professor that afternoon, there had been some sinister overtone about him that had made her feel uneasy in his presence, some hint of the Prince of Darkness that convinced her this was an evil man.

But he was obviously a kind father who took genuine pride in his lovely daughter. And also Elizabeth had seemed quite happy to accept him into her home. Of course her younger brother, Roger, had demurred, but he was always taking the opposite side of everything.

Victoria asked her employer, "Do you think Linda wants to talk to me? She seems rather distant in her manner."

Elizabeth sighed. "She had led such an unusual life. I don't think the girl is at all sure of herself except when she's on stage. Then she has her father to sustain her. I think it would be a kindness on your part to at least attempt to entertain her."

"I'll try," Victoria said and made her way out of the kitchen. As she walked along the corridor leading to the front of the mansion she considered what her probable relationship would be with this girl.

Even though Elizabeth had attempted to make Linda's interest in Ernest seem unimportant, Victoria was by no means sure this was the case. And with the young concert violinist soon returning to Collinwood for a holiday, they would both be thrown in his company. Victoria could find Linda a genuine rival for his affections. She did not want this kind of rivalry and at the same time she hoped to be fair to the other girl.

When she entered the living room, Linda was standing staring up at the portrait of the grim-faced old Jeremiah Collins, who had built Collinwood. As Victoria moved close to her, the girl turned with a cynical expression on her pretty face.

She told Victoria, "When I was very young Dad used to scare me by telling me Jeremiah would come stalking after me if I wasn't a good girl. He's such an ugly old man, I think I could be still frightened by the warning."

Victoria smiled. "Still, he must have been quite a distinguished person. He built this house and founded the business that has made the family so wealthy."

Linda swung around with her hands clasped behind her back. "And made his young French wife so happy she killed herself by jumping over the cliff on Widow's Hill."

"He may not have been to blame."

"With his kind of face, I'd say so," Linda observed. "He always strikes me as having been a cruel man. I don't doubt that some of it has come down through the generations. Even Roger has a nasty streak."

"You seem to take a great interest in the family."

"Why shouldn't I? I've been here so many times over the years, it is like my home." The girl stared at her. "Dad thinks you look like me."

"I don't think there's any great resemblance," Victoria protested, somewhat untruthfully.

"But he is very sharp about such things," Linda said, still studying her. "I guess we are the same type. And you have long black hair exactly like mine."

"You must lead a very interesting life."

Linda looked bored. "Not really. We do the same show every night and often I have no one to take me around in the daytime and show me the different places we visit. So I just sit alone in my hotel room while Daddy talks to cronies in the lobby."

"Your father is an unusual man," Victoria ventured. "Do you think he has any special powers?"

"Of course. He has extrasensory perception. I'm sure of that. His feats of mental telepathy are not all tricks. So many professional mind readers depend on gimmicks and fake routines, but a lot of my father's demonstrations are true examples of reading someone else's mind."

"I've never believed such a thing possible," Victoria confessed.

Linda's arrogant air had returned. She said loftily, "You don't know much about the mind or the spirit world."

"I'll admit to that," Victoria agreed at once.

They were standing close to each other in the semi-darkness of the large living room which was lighted only by an old-fashioned oil lamp on the mantel above the fireplace adjacent to the portrait of Jeremiah Collins. The soft glow of the rose-shaded lamp did not extend far beyond them and left the balance of the huge room a mass of shadows.

"My dad has been hired to investigate haunted houses. He is an authority on such things." Linda turned to leave the room, but over her shoulder she remarked, "You'll learn that he has special powers." And with that she went out and upstairs.

Victoria watched her as she went, wondering if Linda's words had some hidden meaning. It occurred to her that perhaps she had already been a victim of the professor's weird experiments. Or had the phantom she'd encountered on the footpath been a figment of her imagination?

Not long afterward, she and Elizabeth also went up to their respective bedrooms. The storm was still at a high level, although no longer of hurricane force. Victoria swiftly changed into her nightgown and got into the old four-poster bed. She glanced around her familiar room, which seemed oddly different by candlelight, and then blew out the candle and settled down to sleep. But before sleep came she vividly relived that moment when she'd met the Phantom Mariner and the skull face passed grinning before her mind's eye. Her last waking thought was that it had been too real to be imagined.

When she awoke the following morning, the hurricane had ended. But not until she'd had breakfast and gone outside was she aware of the amount of damage that had been done. One of the fine old elms had been uprooted and many of the others had limbs and branches torn from them. One of the many tall chimneys that rose up from the mansard roof of the old house had been half-dismantled. It must have been the bricks from it she'd heard crashing down during the peak of the hurricane. The tide was still abnormally high and there was a brisk, cool breeze. But the sun was shining and the sky was almost devoid of clouds. The bright sunlight sharply revealed the litter and messy state of the lawns.

The dour Matt Morgan was already out with a wheelbarrow, cleaning up. He gave her a disgusted look.

"Man doesn't know where to begin trying to put things to rights!" She stared around her in wonder. "And it all happened in such a short space of time!"

"It'll take a good deal longer for one to do anything about it unless they want to hire some extra help," Matt said harshly as he lifted the handles of his wheelbarrow and trucked the first lot of debris away.

Victoria went on to the path that followed the line of the cliffs and led directly to the high point of Widow's Hill where there was a lookout and a bench. The waves still bore a goodly number of white caps and she guessed it must be rough out there. She turned her eyes from the ocean and saw a strange, dark-clad figure coming toward her at quite a fast walk. It was the bony frame of Professor

Veno outlined against the blue sky. He was wearing the wide-brimmed black hat of the previous day and as he approached her he removed it and bowed.

"What a delightful morning after the storm," he remarked in his smooth voice. The gleam in his eyes as they fixed on her made her wonder if he wasn't versed in hypnosis as well. Very likely he was.

She looked across to Collinwood to avoid his eyes. "I see we have a damaged chimney."

"It could have been much worse," the professor said. "Elizabeth tells me she has a tenant in the cottage."

Once again Victoria marveled at his familiarity with her employer and the casual way in which he used her name. "Yes. She came some weeks ago. She's not well and doesn't have any visitors."

"Surely she would find it hard to discover a more remote place," the professor said, standing with his bald head uncovered and allowing the breeze to blow his wisps of black hair this way and that.

"We believe she has not long to live."

"And she has come here to die alone."

"Except for her manservant."

Professor Veno nodded. "Well, I find it understandable. Even animals want to slink off and die in some dark, deserted place away from those that are close to them. In this case I suppose the cottage is serving its purpose for the poor woman."

"I think so," Victoria agreed.

His eyes burned into her. "You must find this quite different from the life you knew in the city."

"Not too much," she said. "I lived very quietly. I taught at an orphanage."

"Yes," he said, his eyes still probing her in that strange way. "And you yourself are an orphan, isn't that so?"

"Yes," she said in a low voice, trying to elude that terrible stare.

"Elizabeth wrote me all about you," he went on. "You have a good friend in Elizabeth. You will do well to stand by her."

"She has been very kind to me." With an effort Victoria forced herself to break the meeting of their eyes and stare down at the grass.

"No doubt she has her reasons," the professor said evenly. As she glanced up in surprise he quickly added, "I meant, she must be lonely a lot of the time here. She requires a companion."

Victoria said, "I must be getting back to the house."

"Don't let me detain you," the professor said with a change of manner, becoming almost genial. "It is very pleasant to have you here. Especially for my daughter. We must talk more another time."

She almost hurried away from him in her desire to escape those burning eyes. They terrified her. She began to believe it was the spell they had cast on her that made her conjure up the vision of the phantom in the storm. She was relieved to enter the cool quiet of the old mansion.

She felt an urgent desire to talk with someone. And her best friend in Collinsport was the returned millionaire, Burke Devlin. She was anxious to tell him about Professor Mark Veno; surely he would know something about their strange guest. Probably Elizabeth would allow her the use of the station wagon to go into the village for a while in the evening. All that was necessary was to phone Burke and ask him if he would be free.

Elizabeth was busy in the kitchen. She looked up from the pie she was preparing for the oven to nod to Victoria. "Were you shocked by the damage?" she asked.

"It was bad enough," she agreed. "Is the phone working yet?"

"Yes," Elizabeth said. "Roger just called me from the office. He says that fishing boat is still missing. It looks as if the three aboard it have been drowned. A tragic business. Otherwise, things aren't too bad at the cannery."

"May I have the station wagon to go in to Collinsport for a little while tonight?"

The older woman looked at her. "Yes, I guess so. As long as the road is properly cleared—and I think it will be by this evening."

"Thanks," Victoria said, and before her employer had time to reconsider she hurried out to the library to put a call through to Burke Devlin. She reached him at his suite in the hotel.

"I thought you might have been blown away," was his greeting over the wire.

"I expected to be, for a while," she confessed with a small laugh. "But somehow we all survived."

"Much damage?"

"Some. But very little of major importance except one fine old tree down."

"Too bad," Burke Devlin said. "The town is quite a mess. Three or four plate glass windows just caved in."

"Are you going to be busy all evening?"

"Why?" he asked. "You thinking about coming in?"

"Yes."

"I'll meet you in the hotel restaurant," he said. "What time?"

"You're sure I won't be keeping you from anything important?" she asked.

"Only my worries and they can wait. How about eight

o'clock?"

"That should be about right. I'd like to help Elizabeth with the dinner dishes before I leave."

"I'll see you then," Devlin said. "You sound sort of on edge. I take it things have been happening out there besides the storm."

"Maybe," she said vaguely.

He chuckled. "You enjoy a mystery, don't you?"

"I find myself facing enough of them," she said. "I'll be at the hotel as close to eight as I can manage."

"I'll be there," he promised.

She hung up with a mild feeling of elation. Just discussing her problems with Burke always made her feel better. He had an easy, sensible approach to most matters. His authority and good sense made her question what had happened in the past to send him away from Collinsport in disgrace and wonder how he'd managed to rehabilitate himself so completely and return as a millionaire, the mystery man of the area. She had never been able to find the full truth about him from anyone. But she didn't care. She considered he had proven himself her friend and she trusted him.

She started upstairs to make the beds and met Linda who was on her way down. The attractive black-haired girl was wearing a scanty bikini, a big straw sun hat and dark glasses. She was carrying a towel and a bulging beach bag.

Pausing, she asked Victoria, "Are there any chairs out yet? I'd like to get some sun."

"Yes. Around to the side. And the sun should be at its best there right now."

Linda looked pleased. "Thanks," she said, and went on down.

Victoria went on to her work with a barely suppressed sigh. Linda was attractive enough in a bathing suit to turn any man's head. Not only that, she had a confident assured manner, despite Elizabeth's picturing her as a frightened little girl. Victoria could see none of this in her.

As she made the beds she pondered on what would happen when Ernest arrived. Would Linda greedily engage all the young man's time? Had the friendship between them progressed enough during their meetings in Spain to make Linda a real threat to her own romance? It would be ridiculous to say she wasn't worried.

Later, toward the end of the afternoon, she decided to go over to the cottage and chat with Margaret Lucas. Victoria had seen the sullen hunchback, Carlos, drive off to Collinsport in the morning for mail and his daily shopping, and had noticed his return a little before noon. Now she felt she would like to spend a relaxed half-hour with the invalid before she began to help Elizabeth with dinner.

When she came to the spot on the path where she had thought she'd seen the Phantom Mariner she paused and glanced around. It was nearer to the cottage than the main house, but not so far that the professor couldn't have assumed a disguise and been out there in time to intercept her. Still wondering about the incident, she walked slowly on to the cottage.

Carlos answered the door again, his face wearing its usual disdain. "You want to talk to her?"

"Yes," Victoria said, waiting on the outer stone step. "Is she feeling well enough to see me?"

He nodded. "Sure, she's okay today."

"Then may I go in?"

Carlos stepped back to allow her to enter, suspicion showing on his ugly countenance. He said, "You got nothing better to do?"

She was used to his unconventional comments and merely smiled slightly. "I guess that must be it."

He pointed to the closed bedroom door. "She's in there."

Victoria left him to advance to the door and knock lightly on it. At once a pleasant, if somewhat weary, female voice invited her to come in. She found the invalid seated in a chair by the open window, looking pale and ill as usual. She was wearing her dark glasses and had a blanket over her knees.

"I'm so glad you could come, my dear," the sick woman said. "I would have liked to talk to you when you so kindly came during the storm last night. But I just wasn't equal to it."

"That didn't matter," Victoria assured her, touched by her frail appearance.

Margaret Lucas motioned to her to take the vacant chair that was almost opposite hers. She smiled as Victoria sat down. "You look tense, my dear. Don't tell me you have new problems."

"A major one, I'm afraid," Victoria confessed.

"Let me hear about it. I insist. You know how much I love to offer advice."

Victoria quickly gave her the facts about Linda and the professor, ending with, "I don't know what to think of them. But I am sure this Linda is after Ernest."

"I find that most amazing," the invalid said. "I thought he loved you."

"I believe he does," Victoria said. "But this Linda is a menace."

Margaret's pale face showed interest. "From what you tell me, she must be a remarkably attractive young woman."

"There is something about her. The flair you'd expect in an

actress."

The invalid nodded. "I see what you mean."

"And her father is actually sinister," Victoria said unhappily. "I suppose I shouldn't say this. But I don't like him at all. In fact he frightens me."

"He doesn't sound appealing," Margaret agreed. "Why do you suppose Mrs. Stoddard was so willing to invite them into her home?"

"That is also a mystery," she admitted. "And they have been guests there many times over the years."

"You suggest this man, this Professor Mark Veno, has some special powers," the invalid said. "You could be only too right. Mrs. Stoddard might be a victim of his hypnotic influence."

"His eyes are weird. He stares at me and I have to work hard to avoid looking at him."

"A wise precaution," the invalid agreed. "You must try to protect yourself against this man until you find out what manner of evil he is up to—if he is. And just what hold he may have on Mrs. Stoddard—if any other than friendship. You mentioned her husband vanished years ago. Could this professor have been a party to that?"

It was a chilling thought and one that hadn't occurred to Victoria. "I suppose he could have," she admitted. "But I don't think so. I can't see Elizabeth in league with a man like him."

"You don't like to think of her in that role," Margaret corrected her in a gentle voice.

She looked down. "I suppose that is it."

"But don't shut your mind to the unpleasant possibility," Margaret said. "It is the unpleasant ones that are all too often true."

"I'll try to keep that in mind," she said nervously.

"While I admire your loyalty to your employer," Margaret went on, "I think you must make yourself think clearly. Your life could be in danger."

She gave the sick woman a troubled glance. "Surely there is no reason that it should be?"

"None that you know at present," the woman said quietly. "But there are many things to be settled before one can fairly evaluate the situation. You know, I think I would like to meet this Linda Veno."

"You would?" Victoria was startled to hear the recluse say this.

Margaret smiled and nodded. "I realize it is a reversal of my usual attitude toward guests. But I find myself caught up in this story and I mean to see the principals and then offer some opinions."

"You're sure it won't be too tiring for you?"

"On the contrary, it might be beneficial," the invalid said. "At least, let us give it a try. If you can persuade this Linda to give some of her tune to a sick old woman, I'll be glad to see her. I leave it to you to handle as you think best."

"I'll mention it to her," Victoria said, "though I can't promise that she'll come."

"I realize that, but at least it's worth a try."

For once Victoria left Margaret Lucas feeling more confused than when she'd arrived. She had come with what was really a romantic problem, and Margaret had warned her that her very life might be in danger. Again she thought of her glimpse of the Phantom Mariner.

Helping Elizabeth with dinner, she temporarily forgot these problems. But once she had finished and sat down at the table, they came rushing back again.

She kept watching her wristwatch to gauge the passing time and be ready to leave the table as soon as she could. The professor was discoursing on his travels in Europe, with Linda sitting quietly and appearing bored. Elizabeth, at the head of the table, showed interest in the discussion, but her brother, Roger, was plainly impatient.

"We did very well in Belgium," the professor reminisced, his sunken eyes glazed very slightly in recollection. "Brussels cheered us again and again."

"I've no interest in Europe," Roger said testily. "Most of the countries are backward and dirty."

Professor Mark Veno frowned. "That is hardly a fair view of the continent."

"Give me the States anytime," Roger snapped. "Europe may be all right for those that have to live there. I know when I'm lucky."

Elizabeth showed distress. "Now, really, Roger!"

"Now really, Roger!" the blond man said nastily, imitating her. "I'm not afraid to call a spade a spade. I figure the professor knows what I mean."

"Whatever I may know, I don't approve of your attitude," Professor Veno said with a sudden surprising sternness in his voice.

Linda's pretty face looked worried. "We can do without arguments, Dad!"

"I will not have lies about Europe shoved down my throat," her father retorted.

Linda flashed a smile at Roger. "I'm certain Roger was only teasing you. Isn't that so, Roger?"

The blond man looked somewhat mollified. "If that's what you want to think, Linda. You know I never argue with you."

"There, you see?" Linda said, pleased with her victory and giving Victoria a glance to show off her triumph.

At that they all rose from the table and Victoria was relieved, because it was getting close to eight. She was also pleased when Elizabeth joined her in the kitchen to tell her, "Now you get on your way at once and I don't want you coming back too late."

"But I can't leave you with all the dirty dishes," Victoria demurred.

Elizabeth smiled. "Just don't think about it. I'll manage. I'd rather see you get an early start."

Victoria didn't want to attract any attention as she left. She had an idea that Roger might interfere and argue against her going in to Collinsport in his present sullen mood. She left by the kitchen door and walked swiftly to the station wagon. As she drove away, she saw Matt Morgan come to the doorway of the barn and stolidly watch her as she headed for the woods road.

It still was a few minutes short of eight. With luck she would be almost in time for her appointment with Burke Devlin. Although the woods road showed washouts and other signs of the storm, it was easily passable. At exactly seven minutes before eight she parked in front of the town's shabby hotel.

As she entered the lobby the distinguished-looking Burke Devlin rose from a leather chair to greet her with a smile. "Well," he observed, "you're that rarity, a woman who almost always arrives in time."

She smiled. "It was a close call tonight."

Burke nodded with understanding. "Did Elizabeth know you were coming here to meet me?"

"I didn't tell her in so many words, but she knows you're one of the few friends I have in Collinsport."

"And I suppose she doesn't much like the idea of you keeping dates with an older man?" he suggested.

Victoria looked at him shyly. "This isn't exactly a date and somehow I never think of you as an older man."

"Well, I'll not try to break that down for meaning," he said with a resigned smile. "Let's go in and order coffee and hear all about your problems." He escorted her into the coffee shop, which was almost deserted. A neon-lighted jukebox was playing in the corner, but it was only loud enough to keep their conversation from being overheard.

After the waitress brought them their coffee, Burke Devlin eyed her across the table. "Maybe we should have gone to the Blue Whale?" he suggested.

"No. This will do. I don't want to stay late. And we might meet Joe or somebody else we know there." Joe, a sometime boyfriend of Carolyn's, made the Blue Whale his headquarters.

"Very well," Burke said without bothering to touch his coffee. "Now let's hear what is on your mind."

"It's pretty complicated," she admitted. "And I may be making a lot out of nothing." And with that she began a recital of the arrival of Professor Mark Veno and his daughter and all that had gone on since. She even included her frightening encounter with the Phantom Mariner.

Burke lifted his eyebrows at this. "You no sooner heard the legend than you went out in the dark and saw the ghost."

She felt embarrassed. "It sounds that way. It didn't happen in quite that quick a sequence."

The man across from her had a thoughtful expression on his handsome, weathered face. "You want to know what I think?"

"Of course."

"I think you may be in for a lot of trouble."

"Oh?"

"For one thing," Burke went on, "this man you've told me about and called Professor Mark Veno is known to me. And his name doesn't happen to be Mark Veno at all!"

CHAPTER 3

Victoria gave him a startled look. "I don't think I understand."
Burke Devlin smiled. "I didn't expect you to. You see, you don't have my advantage of being a native of this area. It's the only way one really gets to know the old families and the hidden skeletons in their closets."

"What has that to do with Professor Mark Veno?"

He put several lumps of sugar in his coffee and slowly stirred it. Then he took a sip and remarked with satisfaction, "I like lots of sugar in my coffee." His eyes held a humorous gleam. "You're dying with curiosity, aren't you?"

"I don't think you're being fair," she protested. "Tell me!"

He put down his cup. "Very well. Let's get it straight from the beginning. Professor Mark Veno's real name is Mark Collins!"

She stared at him incredulously. "He is a Collins!"

"Better than that. He is a full brother to Elizabeth and Roger. In fact, Mark is the older brother."

Victoria was completely confused. "But what does it mean? Why should he be using a different name? And why do they carry on this pretense that he is a friend, rather than a member of the family?"

"It's one of those things that go unsaid," Burke told her seriously. "They are all aware of the situation. Mark has a right to be at Collinwood and there is nothing they can do about it."

"But what is his position in regard to the family?"

Burke smiled. "Now I'll get down to explanations. Mark was the firstborn and the apple of his father's eye. His father had ambitious plans for him, but he didn't reckon on the kind of young man Mark was going to turn out to be. When he came back from Harvard he took his place in the office of the canning company as assistant manager. It was a position created for him by his father while he learned the business."

"But he didn't do well?"

"In a sense he did too well," Burke replied. "He developed an interest in gambling and perfected a system to swindle the firm for his cash needs. And they were far from modest. In the old days there was always a card game under way in one of the rooms on the upper floor of this very hotel. The commercial men who passed through here kept it going and Mark spent his evenings at the card table. Usually he lost. But he was cheerful about it, since there was always more cash where the money had come from."

"I suppose his father eventually caught on."

"It took him quite a while to accept that Mark was a scoundrel. Then he threw him out of the firm and out of his house. It caused quite a scandal. The next word about Mark was that he had turned up in New York. He was still gambling and had earned the reputation of being crooked at cards. It was in this period he wooed and married some poor young girl he met while she was working behind the counter in a department store. Mark has always had a suave manner and no doubt he turned the girl's head with stories of wealth."

"And this girl became Linda's mother?"

"No," Burke said and he took another sip of his coffee. "Mark deserted this girl before her baby was born. And the story goes that mother and child died in childbirth."

"How awful!"

"Awful for the girl, but I don't think it bothered Mark much. He isn't a type to brood. He married again after he had taken up mind reading as a profession—and incidentally he's very good at it. This time he found a wife while on tour in Mexico. She was a fairly wealthy Mexican woman with a fine family background. She gave up everything to become his wife and for some years traveled with him as his assistant in the act. And it was she who became Linda's mother."

"Linda does have a slightly Latin look and bearing," Victoria agreed, fascinated by the story.

Burke nodded. "But this second marriage was not destined to turn out happily either. Mark no longer had to cheat at cards to make a living. He was cured of his gambling and completely absorbed with the mentalism which had become his profession. Unlike most stage mentalists, he made a thorough study of the mind and developed his natural abilities in the field in a scientific way. But as he became more expert as a mind reader he also grew more eccentric and withdrawn. As a husband he became a cold, cruel person to live with. So in the end his wife began to despise him."

"And this led to a divorce?"

"Not directly. She was unfaithful to him and it was he who instigated the divorce action and received custody of Linda. He and his wife parted hating each other. And Mark continued to be vindictive, raising the little girl entirely on his own and making sure that as soon as she was old enough she was told the story of her mother's desertion of her."

Burke paused. "That is the kind of person Mark is. He meant that Linda should grow up hating her mother."

"I don't like him at all," she confessed. "I'm sure he is an accomplished hypnotist. His eyes scare me."

"You may be right," Burke said. "At any rate, he has been a good father to Linda in his own way. And I imagine she adores him."

"She does."

"And Linda will inherit a large share of the Collins estate in due time. By the terms of her grandfather's will the fortune will be divided among the surviving grandchildren when Elizabeth and Roger have died. If Linda is alive she will come into her full share of the money. In the meantime, she and her father have no Collins money, but they do have the privileges of the house whenever they wish to stay there. Neither Elizabeth nor Roger can turn them away. It's all set down in the will."

"What an amazing story!" she said.

Burke Devlin's smile was mocking. "But then, Collinwood is a truly amazing house."

"You don't have to tell me that," Victoria said with a frown. "Often I wish I had never seen it."

"Then you would have never met me."

She smiled faintly. "And that would have been too bad. But so much has happened since I've been there. And so many things are still a mystery to me. Now you tell me this weird story about Mark Collins and admit he is a strange, cruel man."

"He is all that. But at least you have been warned about him."

Victoria's pretty face wore a look of utter perplexity. "How am I to behave? Will I let Elizabeth and the others know that I'm aware of Professor Mark Veno's true identity? Make it plain that I've found out he is one of the family?"

He shook his head. "No. I think you should go along with their charade. Even among themselves they have grown accustomed to the arrangement of looking on Mark as a friend rather than a brother. Linda regards Elizabeth and Roger as older people interested in her and not as her uncle and aunt, even though she knows the truth and that she will one day own a part of the Collins estate."

"I'll try to remember," Victoria said with a worried air. "It won't be easy knowing what I do."

"I'd simply avoid Mark as much as possible," Burke advised her.

"But he seems to go out of his way to seek my company."

"I see," he said thoughtfully. "Well, be assured of one thing, he must have a reason."

"I think I know what it could be," she hazarded.

"Oh?"

"He wants Ernest for his daughter," she said. "And he very likely has the idea I'm standing in the way."

Burke Devlin gave a low whistle. "I'd forgotten about Linda's friendship with Ernest. At least, I didn't take much stock of it when you mentioned it. Now I see it could play a part in what's happening."

"Ernest is expected very shortly."

"And you think Mark is anxious to promote the romance between Linda and him."

"I'm certain of it."

Burke showed concern. "But Ernest has never mentioned Linda to you?"

"No."

"So he can't have felt his friendship with her had any importance. I mean, he has talked to you seriously about the possibility of marriage. Surely if Linda meant anything in his life, he'd have mentioned her before this."

"I would have hoped so," she said carefully, still filled with unhappy doubts. Was it possible this romance between Ernest and Linda had been a whirlwind thing? That he had put off explaining about it until he had a chance to talk to her on his return?

Burke studied her in silence for a few seconds. "You are a little worried, aren't you?"

Victoria bit her lip and sighed. "I'm afraid so."

"I think you're wrong," the millionaire said shortly. "I know Ernest and I've always found him a sincere person. I don't think he'd be capable of changing his mind so quickly, of giving way to a quick flirtation."

"Even if that is true, if Ernest still loves me," she said, "I could be in a difficult position with regard to Mark. He would see me as a stumbling block to Linda's romance."

"Of course," Burke agreed seriously. "And to a person of his cold, determined type that would suggest one thing. Eliminating you."

Victoria was only too well aware of that. She sat back in her chair as the jukebox gave out with a weird, chanted vocal full of eerie electronic effects. It throbbed in her brain, a hopeless, despairing distillation of young love, and the bizarre dirge seemed to fit her mood exactly. She glanced at the several teen-age couples seated at tables near the neon-lighted jukebox and noted the rapt, dazed looks on their faces as they listened to the music.

She was silent for a few moments, her eyes wandering about the softly-lighted room in which the thundering jukebox stood out with its bright yellow, green and blue tubing. What kind of new trouble was she facing at Collinwood? And had Ernest, whom she counted on above anyone else, betrayed her?

Leaning forward again, she said, "I think Mark Collins has already made an attempt to frighten me away. He brought up that legend of the Phantom Mariner and then made himself up to look like the ghost and came out to accost me along the path."

"Did you tell Elizabeth about it?"

"No, I didn't like to. I was sure she'd think I was hysterical. That the ghost story and the night had worked on my nerves."

"But you do believe you saw the phantom?"

She looked directly at him. "I can still picture that awful skull face and the cowl framing it."

"You make it sound real enough."

"It did happen! And I know it was the professor who was responsible. I think he is half mad."

Burke Devlin smiled wryly. "Maybe even more than that." He paused. "So you must take special care. When will Ernest be arriving?"

"No one is sure. But it will be soon."

"You'll be glad to see him and have a talk," Burke suggested. "At least it will ease some of your tension."

"I would like to know the truth," she admitted. "Just how much Linda does mean to him."

"As I mentioned before, I wouldn't worry about it," Burke said. "Still, it will be good to have Ernest back and there to keep an eye on you. It is also possible that Mark Collins won't remain at the house too long. He seldom does."

"This time he'll at least wait until Ernest arrives," she

pointed out.

"Undoubtedly," Burke agreed. "And in the meantime, don't hesitate to call on me. Keep me informed of anything unusual that happens."

"I owe you so much already," she said. "From the time I've arrived here you've been my friend."

His handsome face showed a smile. "It has been more than a one-sided affair," he assured her. "I've taken a great deal of pleasure in your company."

"Burke, why did Elizabeth bring me here in the first place?" she demanded ruefully.

He looked surprised. "To look after young David."

"That was her excuse," she argued. "I don't see it as the real reason. So much is hidden in that house. And now I find there is an older brother." She paused. "You mentioned that he was married before he took Linda's mother as his wife. And you said the girl died in childbirth? Suppose she died and her baby lived? And that Mark Collins left it at an orphanage to be rid of it?"

The millionaire frowned. "Now don't start getting ideas again."

"But honestly, Burke, it could be that way," she said excitedly. "I could have been that baby he deserted years ago. His unwanted child! And perhaps the only one who knows about it is Elizabeth! That's why the money was sent from Bangor to the orphanage and why I was finally brought here by her. It was her way of making amends!"

"It's fancy theorizing," Burke Devlin admitted, "and it could even be possible. But I'll ask you just one thing. Does Mark Collins seem like a father to you?"

"No! He repels me!"

"Exactly," Burke said as he waved to the waitress for their check. "And that is my argument against your theory. If Mark Collins was your father you'd feel quite differently toward him."

"Even if he was a father who deserted me? Left me a helpless infant on the steps of an orphanage?"

"I think so," he said. "Still, I could be wrong." He paid for their coffee and then saw her out to the station wagon. After again insisting that she keep in touch with him, he stood back and waited for her to drive away.

She waved as she turned the corner and headed back to the main road. As soon as she was alone again she lost the feeling of assurance she'd known while in Burke Devlin's company. The mystery millionaire of Collinsport had a way of making her relaxed and optimistic. But now she was alone and faced with the reality of her position. And the reality wasn't all that encouraging.

Mark Collins, whom she kept on thinking of as the professor, had a kind of obsession where his daughter was concerned. Victoria felt that he would do anything for Linda. His main desire was to see his daughter happy. And what better way to ensure that than to have her marry Ernest Collins. She was certain the professor would ruthlessly attempt to remove anything or anyone who stood in the way of such a match.

And as she drove along in the darkness, her eyes fixed on that portion of the road ahead exposed by the beam of her headlights, she worried about it all. Burke was right in at least one thing. She would need to take care.

She was also concerned about the matter of her parentage again. The story about Mark Collins had revived it to torment her. While she was loath to think of the repulsive man as her father, she knew it just might happen to be the truth.

The road was almost deserted. When she turned into the side road that led through the woods to Collinwood, she was completely alone. Few cars used that road. Avoiding the washouts, she drove carefully, not wanting to have an accident.

At last she was through the trees and Collinwood stood out against the dark sky ahead. There were still a few scattered lights showing in its windows. She parked the car in the rear with the others and started to walk around to the front door, which she always used at this time of night.

A glance upward told her there were a few stars overhead, with the promise that the next day might be fine again. At this period in September the days could be as warm and pleasant as at any time in the summer. After such a storm, the weather might be good for a while.

She was nearing the front of the house when a startling sound came to her—a moan from directly behind her. With a troubled frown she halted and listened. There was the distant, regular wash of the waves on the shore and the eerie nocturnal croaking of frogs, and then above those normal night noises there came the moan again. This time it was loud and distinct.

Victoria turned with a feeling of alarm. Someone must be in desperate trouble. Standing where she was, she called out, "Who is it?"

She waited. There was no reply. The night seemed suddenly menacing. She decided to go into the house and report what she'd heard to whoever might be awake. She took a step toward the house when there was another moan. This time she turned and walked backward several steps, peering into the darkness and in the areas of the tall ornamental shrubbery that surrounded the house.

Suddenly, without warning, something dropped over her head! A loop slid around her neck and was quickly tightened by someone behind her. The someone at the same time propelled her forward. Victoria tried to call out, but couldn't. The cord, or whatever it was, bit into her throat and threatened to cut off all breath. She clawed frantically to free herself and then felt the earth give way under her feet. She was over the brink of some precipice!

She made another attempt to scream as she fell but only a hoarse, choked sound emerged. Frantically she reached out in an effort to stay her fall, having no idea where she was or what happened. Her hands touched rocks, cold and slimy. She sought for a hold and found a precarious one. Now, miraculously, her fall was broken but she was immersed in total darkness, close to unconsciousness and her hands felt strained and torn as she clung to her precarious hold on the slippery rocks.

Sheer desperation made her call out again. And this time her scream was near normal in volume. Encouraged that she could at least make herself heard, she continued to scream. Again and again she shrieked as her hands slipped ever so little on the wet rocks and she felt she must drop to her death.

From a great distance away there was the thud of footsteps. And then a concerned male voice shouted, "What's going on?"

"Victoria!" she cried her name frantically. "Please help me!"

"What the blazes!" The voice came from directly above her and it was Roger's. Then hastily, "Just a moment!" There was the sound of footsteps retreating.

She clung there, the pain in her hands agonizing, her shoulders aching from strain. And now she knew where she was! In the well! The old abandoned well that was located close to the house. It was kept covered and once Ernest had rescued her from walking over a dangerously old wooden covering, but it had been replaced shortly after that. Tonight someone had attacked her and deliberately shoved her into the well. After the torrential rains of the hurricane it was undoubtedly near full of water. If she had dropped all the way into its murky depths she might have been drowned as her attacker intended.

She wished Roger would hurry. She could not hold on much longer!

Then Roger's voice came close once more and it mingled with that of Matt Morgan's. After what seemed an endless time the bright beam of a flashlight shone down the mouth of the dank, mossy well, blinding her.

"Hold on!" Roger's tone was encouraging. "Just a few minutes longer."

"I'll try," she murmured between teeth gritted from

physical pain. She knew they could not have heard her but it helped her to reply—made it seem that there had been a contact between them.

There were scuffling sounds from above and then she knew someone else was slowly being lowered into the circular, stonewalled old well. She moved slightly and was further terrified as she almost lost her grip.

"Take it easy!" Roger said, and he was close beside her now. She felt his body brush against hers and then his arm grasped her. Even though he had taken the weight of her body, the desperate urge for self-preservation still made her cling madly to the slimy, uneven rocks. "It's all right! Let go now!" he commanded her.

With a frightened sob she let her hands relax at the same instant that he began the return journey up the well. It took a long while and she could hear the man above straining to take in the rope and bring them to the surface.

Then hands reached out for her and pulled her to safety on the wet grass and she heard Roger and Matt Morgan uttering grateful oaths that the ordeal was over. She lay there panting and sick with fear.

The flashlight flooded her again and Roger was kneeling by her. "You're safe enough now," he said. "What happened? How did you get in there?"

"I don't know," she moaned, raising on an elbow. "I heard someone groaning. I went to see who it was. The next thing I knew I was being pushed into the well!"

"More likely stumbled into it!" Roger said with disgust. "Some damned fool had the covering off and left it off. Did you have anything to do with it, Morgan?"

"I wasn't near the well," Morgan said quickly.

"Well, someone must have been," Roger maintained. "There are always a few youngsters from the village straying over the grounds during the daytime."

"Like as not one of them took the cover off the well to see if the storm filled it and left it off," Matt Morgan pointed out indignantly.

"Even if that's what happened, you should have noticed," Roger rebuked him.

"I'm only one man. I can't take care of everything," Morgan said with some anger.

"Well, you've seen the result! Victoria might have been killed," Roger said. Turning to her, he asked, "Do you think you can stand up now?"

She nodded. "Yes."

He assisted her to her feet. "That was a close call. It was just one chance in a thousand that you managed to grasp those rocks and hold on."

She closed her eyes. "I couldn't imagine what had happened. I didn't know where I was. I kept falling!" She was trembling with shock and felt nauseated.

"Don't think about it now," Roger said, with a consideration surprising in him. She was suddenly aware that he had conducted himself in this crisis with unusual level-headedness. He began to guide her toward the front door.

Elizabeth, in her dressing gown, was waiting just inside. Her attractive face showed alarm as she saw the state Victoria was in. "What ever is the matter?" she said, taking her in her arms.

"Covering was off the well and she stumbled into it," Roger said. "I've said for years that well should be filled in."

"And yet you've done nothing about it," Elizabeth retorted angrily. "Help me get her upstairs."

Victoria heard all this in a vague, meaningless way. She felt a grim weariness seep through her. Nothing seemed to matter.

At last she was in her own room and safely in bed. Elizabeth sat at her bedside with a basin and was bathing her hands. The older woman's sensitive face showed concern. "You've broken nearly all your fingernails and torn the palms of your hands!"

Victoria was conscious of the pain in them. "I had to hold on," she murmured.

"You did exactly right," Elizabeth agreed. "But what were you doing by the well? You didn't have to walk near it coming from the car."

Victoria looked up at her. "I heard someone out there groan. I went to see who it was."

Elizabeth frowned incredulously. "Someone groaned out there and attracted your attention."

"Yes. I went over. Something looped around my neck and tightened. I almost passed out. Then I was pushed forward into the well!"

Elizabeth's lovely eyes widened with fear. "You're saying someone deliberately tried to murder you?"

"I'm sure of it."

The older woman was obviously incredulous. She sat there frozen by the announcement. Finally she murmured, "But that just isn't possible!"

"It couldn't have happened any other way," Victoria told her.

"But Roger said someone had left the covering off the well and you'd just happened to stumble into it."

"He took that for granted. It's what he wanted to believe since it was the most obvious explanation."

Elizabeth stared at her. "You didn't mention this to him at all, then?"

"I told him. But he didn't listen. Or, at least, he didn't seem to believe me."

The older woman nodded. "That's typical of Roger."

Victoria raised herself on an elbow, her fear mirrored in her eyes. "But that is how it happened."

"I'm ready to believe you," Elizabeth assured her, with a strangely troubled expression on her lovely face.

"Why should anyone want to kill me?" Victoria asked. And she waited now to hear if Elizabeth would reveal the truth about her brother. Surely the pseudo-professor was the most likely suspect.

Elizabeth drew a deep breath. "That's a question not easily answered," she said. "I don't think there is anyone here who would want to harm you. It could be the work of some stranger. Someone loitering on the estate. We do get undesirables occasionally."

Victoria listened with growing alarm. Elizabeth was not going to be frank with her. She was evading any mention of her brother Mark and attempting to shift the blame to someone outside the house. In spite of the older woman's kindness, she felt betrayed. Deliberately she said, "Perhaps you should let the Collinsport police know."

"I don't believe so," Elizabeth responded too quickly. "I'll think it all over and decide in the morning."

Victoria looked at her directly. "You're afraid they'll put my story down as the raving of a hysterical female?"

"In a way," Elizabeth agreed. "And also I hesitate to bring the police into it until we're very sure. So much has happened here! We've been the subject of so much notoriety and gossip. I'm sure you understand."

Victoria looked down at her injured hands. "Of course I'll do whatever you say," she said quietly.

The note of sad resignation in her voice must have touched the older woman, for Elizabeth reached out and placed a hand on her shoulder. "Don't think I'm not concerned about this. I am! It's just that I'd like to look after it in my own way."

Victoria was sure she knew what Elizabeth had in mind. She would quietly sound out her brother and decide whether she thought he was guilty or not before taking any action. Wanting to see how the older woman would react, she deliberately asked, "Isn't it strange that my cries woke neither the professor nor his daughter?"

Elizabeth looked uneasy. "They're both on the other side of the house," was her explanation. "Roger luckily happened to be downstairs and I'm a light sleeper." She rose with the basin. "There's nothing more to be done for your hands. Do you think it would be safe if I left you now?"

"I'm sure I'll be quite safe," Victoria said with irony as she lay back on the pillow. She closed her eyes and waited for Elizabeth to leave, sick at what she felt was this latest betrayal.

CHAPTER 4

Victoria had read somewhere that murderers suffer a compulsion to return to the scene of their crime. The next morning was warm and sunny again and as soon as she'd finished breakfast she found herself restless to go out and survey the area around the old well. She considered this an instance where a surviving victim was unable to resist revisiting the scene of an attack.

She had several reasons for wanting to study the section in which the well was located. One was to locate where the groaning had come from. When she went out to the well, she found Matt Morgan at work nailing down the plank covering. Standing by him, watching with cynical amusement, was the swarthy hunchback, Carlos Marelli.

Seeing her, Matt straightened and mopped his perspiring brow. The handyman snapped, "Nobody is going to get this open again without some work."

"It's a relief to know that," she said. "It has always been a hazard."

Matt eyed her darkly. "There's some around here can get into trouble, no matter what you do!" And he got down on his knees again and resumed nailing the covering in place.

Victoria knew that from the time of her arrival at the old mansion, the big, gruff Matt had taken a dislike to her. And having this extra task to perform on her account wasn't increasing her popularity with him.

Carlos edged over to her with a sneering smile on his ugly face. He nodded toward the well. "So you jumped in there last night?"

"Not quite," she said evenly.

"You were lucky to get out, eh?" He was staring at her.

"I suppose I was."

He indicated her hands. "Pretty fingers took some punishment," he said in his softly accented voice.

She crimsoned as she gazed down at her broken nails and the cuts and raw spots where the sharp rocks had taken their toll. Yet, thanks to the bathing Elizabeth had given her hands, they didn't look too awful and weren't terribly painful.

The hunchback seemed to enjoy the embarrassment he was causing her. "A girl like you ought to get wise," Carlos said.

She frowned at the strange little man in his gray chauffeur's uniform and cap. "What do you mean?" she asked.

"You got a nice neck. Look after it," Carlos said with a grin.

"I'm afraid I don't follow you," Victoria replied, not bothering to hide her impatience.

"You ought to get a long distance away from here," the hunchback told her. "To a healthier climate!" And with that he grinned again and walked away.

She stared at him as he headed for the cottage with his peculiar swaying gait. How much did he know? Had he some idea of who had attacked her last night? And then she had a new and startling thought. Suppose he was the one who had lured her into the darkness and then tried to kill her? But then, why would he want to?

And she wasn't ready to transfer her suspicions from Mark Collins as yet. He was much too likely a suspect. With a sigh she left Matt Morgan still busy working on the well and went back into the house.

Elizabeth was finishing the breakfast dishes in the kitchen. She looked up from the dishpan as Victoria entered and warned her, "I don't want you thinking about work at all today."

"I'm perfectly all right," Victoria insisted.

"Wait another day until your hands are better."

"I won't know what to do with myself," she protested.

Elizabeth smiled. "Don't try to tell me that. You can talk with Linda. Enjoy the sun. And you're always welcome at the cottage. Mrs. Lucas will be glad to see you."

"I was talking to her chauffeur by the well just now." Victoria said. "He's an odd person."

"I don't think he understands English at all, even though he doesn't speak it too badly."

"That may be it," she worried. "I only know he always seems to be taunting me about something. There's nothing friendly in his manner."

"I've noticed his bitterness," Elizabeth agreed as she emptied the water from the dishpan into the sink. "It could be because of his affliction."

"He seemed to know all about last night," she went on. "And I had the idea he wasn't too sympathetic."

Elizabeth gave her a quick glance. "You're not suggesting he had something to do with your fall?"

"It wasn't a fall!" Victoria knew there was an edge of impatience in her tone.

"Well, whatever it was," Elizabeth said lamely. "You don't think he was the one who lured you into the dark to attack you?"

"It could have been anyone," she admitted. "I didn't even get a glimpse of the person."

"Unfortunate!"

"I agree," she said. "Have you decided about the police?"

"Give me a little longer to think it out," Elizabeth said vaguely.

"If you like," she said. She hadn't expected any quick decision from her employer. It was doubtful whether she'd had a chance to talk with Mark yet. She added, "Have you seen the professor this morning?"

"Very briefly. He's gone for a walk."

Victoria's eyes met those of the older woman. "Did he seem surprised about last night?"

Elizabeth hesitated for only a moment. "I just mentioned it to him. He thought it an unfortunate accident."

"I see," she said ironically.

"Don't think I'm taking the incident lightly," Elizabeth assured her. "I intend to look into it fully. Now, why don't you go on out and get some sun while you have the chance?"

"Thanks," she said listlessly. She left the kitchen and started up to her room. It hurt her to feel Elizabeth would sacrifice her in an effort to protect her brother Mark. From Victoria's point of view, this was what the older woman was doing.

In her room Victoria changed quickly into a pair of dark shorts and a matching halter. Finding her sunglasses and a tube of lotion she then went back downstairs again and to the patio where the chairs were set out. Linda was already there stretched lazily on her stomach, her feet up in the air as she leaned on an elbow to read a paperback.

She turned when Victoria came out and said, "I didn't think you'd be feeling well enough to be around today."

Victoria held up her hands. "They received the worst damage!" She dragged a bench over close to the one Linda was on and sat down.

Linda was showing new interest in her. "What an awful thing to have happen! I'm glad it wasn't me."

Victoria was rubbing some sun lotion on. She said, "I wouldn't want to go through it again."

"I saw the handyman nailing down the covering of the well, so you're not liable to. Did you have a pleasant evening in town last night?"

Victoria shrugged. "Collinsport isn't exactly an exciting place, especially now that the tourist season is over. I met a friend and we had coffee at the hotel restaurant and talked."

Behind her dark sunglasses Linda made a face. "You did better than me. I was stuck here with Roger Collins and Dad. They were full of talk about the old days in the town. I couldn't care less!"

"Didn't Elizabeth keep you company at all?"

"You know how strange she can be," Linda said, glancing at the house. "She went upstairs early. Don't you think it's absolute nonsense, her never leaving Collinwood for years simply because her husband disappeared?"

"I really have no opinion about it."

Linda stared at her. "You mean it's not diplomatic for someone in your place to notice her oddness. I suppose you're wise."

Victoria would have liked to have told the girl that there were many other odd things to which she'd been careful to close her eyes—such as that Professor Mark Veno was really Mark Collins and that she was Linda Collins, niece to Elizabeth and Roger. But she liked Linda and had no desire to hurt her. So instead she said, "I try to mind my own business."

Linda was stretched out on her side, leaning her head on a hand as she studied Victoria. "That's a good quality," she said. "I've felt from the first you are a person to be trusted."

Victoria smiled. "I don't know about that."

"I'm serious," Linda insisted. "Dad was going on again last night about how much we look alike. I believe it bothers him."

"Why should it?" She was interested in finding out more about the supposed professor and had an idea, his daughter might be able to supply some interesting facts if properly led on.

"My father is a strange man," Linda said, frowning. "But then, I guess you've noticed that. But not only is he peculiar in his dress, he happens to have obsessions."

"In what sense?"

"He gets ideas about things and won't change them," Linda said with a sigh. "For example, he thinks Berlin is a very bad place for our mental act and he refuses to allow his agents to book us there even though we've been offered fabulous sums. And he won't allow a man or woman with red hair to come on the stage as a subject anywhere! Redheads are taboo!"

Victoria laughed. "I think that's funny!"

"Perhaps it is," the other girl said. "But not if you have to live with it all the time. You don't really know the kind of man my father is at all. You couldn't guess."

Victoria had the feeling the girl was close to revealing that her father was really a Collins and she didn't want to appear to encourage her. She merely said, "I'd say your father was a very complex individual. It's likely why he's a success in his work."

"His work!" Linda said disgustedly. "All he cares about is his work! The only bit of fun I've had was when we met Ernest Collins in Spain last year and then again last month." She gave another big sigh. "I hope he soon gets here."

"He shouldn't be long coming now," she said.

"Dad doesn't consider anyone but himself! I think that is why my mother ran away from him ages ago." She glanced quickly at Victoria. "She did! And I don't blame her, although that's what he wants."

"I suppose it's natural he should be jealous of your affections under the circumstances," Victoria ventured.

"And he is jealous!" Linda declared. "For years he tried to make out she was dead. And then Agnes, who used to take care of me, told me different. She gave me my mother's address. Since then I've been writing to her. She lives in Paris. She's a wonderful person!"

"Does your father have any idea you've been corresponding with her?"

"He'd be wild if he knew!" Linda declared. "But I'm going to go on writing to her just the same. She is my mother and I love her. I've never seen her since I was a baby, but I mean to when we return to Europe."

"Won't that be difficult?"

"Not too hard," Linda explained. "We're playing in Paris for a month. I'll be able to slip away from Dad a few times at least. And I mean to. I want to get to know my mother."

Victoria smiled. "I don't blame you for that."

"I thought you'd understand. My father said Elizabeth wrote him you were an orphan."

"That is so," Victoria agreed quietly.

"So you know what it means to hunger for a parent."

"I do."

Linda brightened. "You've met Ernest, of course?"

"Yes, we've met here," Victoria said, finding the conversation growing increasingly difficult.

"I wrote mother about him when I was in Spain," Linda confessed somewhat coyly. "I told her that he was the first man I'd ever felt I'd like to marry. She was impressed and asked me all about him in her next letter."

"That was natural."

Linda sighed happily. "So I tried to describe him. And honestly, I think putting down my thoughts about him on paper only made my crush worse. Mother was delighted with my description of Ernest and said she thought I was perfectly right in wanting to marry him. So there!"

Victoria sat up. "I think I'll go in now," she said, by way of excusing herself. "I don't want to stay out too long in the sun at one time."

Linda looked disappointed. "And we were just beginning to have such a nice chat!"

"We'll talk some more later," Victoria promised as she got up. "I've enjoyed it."

She went inside feeling guilty and unhappy. She had deliberately let the somewhat naive Linda tell a good many of her secrets. Even if Linda should be a serious rival for Ernest's affections, Victoria couldn't dislike her. And what had been said just now made her wonder just how serious the affair between Linda and Ernest had been. Of course, she was hearing it only from Linda's point of view. And Linda, by her own admission, was a love-struck and starry-eyed girl where the young violinist was concerned.

The hall was deserted. Remembering her promise to keep Burke Devlin informed of what was happening at the old mansion, she decided to try to reach him on the phone before she went upstairs. She quickly dialed the number of the hotel and asked for his suite.

After a moment's delay the hotel operator said, "I'm sorry, Mr. Devlin doesn't seem to be in. Is there any message?"

"No," Victoria said. "I'll call again." And she put the phone down with disappointment shadowing her pretty face. She had wanted to tell him about her narrow escape in the well. But it would have to wait.

In spite of Elizabeth's protests she insisted on helping her prepare lunch. At one o'clock they all gathered at the dining room table. Roger had come home early from the office and already was showing the effects of several martinis.

Professor Veno, dressed in his usual sober black, smiled from his place at the foot of the table. "I had a fine walk around the estate this morning," he announced.

Elizabeth showed a pleasant interest. "Did you notice many changes?"

"Not really," the professor said, his bony face thoughtful. "But then, it's not long since we made our last visit."

"More than a year, Dad," Linda reminded him.

"And you've grown into a beautiful filly in that time," Roger said gallantly as he paused over his salad.

Professor Veno's deep-set eyes showed annoyance. "I suppose I am more interested in the historical side of the estate. I spent some time standing at the point from which Jeremiah Collins' wife Josette hurled herself into the ocean."

Roger threw his fork down on his plate with an exasperated groan. He glared at the mentalist. "Is that the most lively subject you can think of for luncheon small talk?"

Mark Veno smiled sarcastically. "I had no idea you possessed such delicate feelings, Roger."

"A man doesn't have to be especially delicate to want to avoid discussing century-old suicides!"

The professor shrugged. "Perhaps you would prefer that I mention the suicide of that unhappy young woman artist from the same spot a few years ago."

"I don't want to talk about suicides at all," Roger said angrily as he resumed eating.

"Professor Veno doesn't mean to annoy you, Roger," Elizabeth said in a tone of gentle reproval.

"He does just the same," Roger snapped.

"I agree," Linda said, with a small smile for Victoria. "I say Dad is entirely too morbid."

"Do you agree, Miss Winters?" Professor Veno asked, the strange eyes gleaming at her. "Am I to be left without any supporters?"

Somewhat flustered, Victoria said, "I'm afraid I haven't really been listening."

"Too bad," he told her. "But then, I imagine you haven't fully recovered from your dreadful accident last night. I'd judge you are still not yourself, as a result of the shock."

"I'm not feeling too bad," she said, avoiding those eyes.

Roger glanced up. "She'd have damned well drowned if I

hadn't heard her and got out there in time to save her!"

Victoria smiled gratefully. "And I appreciate it."

"I'm not worried about appreciation," Roger snapped. "But I would like to get my hands on the damned puppy who lifted that covering and left it off!"

"There's no need for such violent language, Roger," Elizabeth chided him. "Victoria escaped without too much damage and we have seen to it that the covering can't be removed in the future."

"I'm glad to hear that," Professor Veno said in his suave, mocking way. "And I'm certain Miss Winters is, as well. But to get back to my own wanderings this morning. I was fascinated by that lonely point of land which has been a favorite spot for suicides. And I couldn't help wondering what their mental states might have been to compel them to throw themselves down on those cruel rocks."

"You should certainly know more about that than any of us," Elizabeth pointed out.

"Of course I admit to that," the man in black agreed. "As I stood there I attempted to project myself into the minds of those unfortunates. To imitate their thoughts in the moments before they leaped to their deaths."

"Impossible to do that," Roger stated firmly.

"I think I managed fairly well," the professor assured him. "You see, I do understand the most devious twists of the human mind."

"Then you should know I've heard enough on the matter," Roger said, folding his napkin angrily and tossing it on the table by his plate. "Tomorrow we can discuss some other pleasant subject, like grave robbing!" He got up in a rage and strode out of the dining room.

The professor raised his thin eyebrows. "There are times when I worry about Roger's blood pressure."

Lunch ended on this note. Victoria was more firmly convinced than ever that her attacker of the previous night had been Professor Mark Veno, alias Mark Collins, the errant son of the family. She was certain he had been mocking her and Roger at lunch, tormenting them in his superior way. She avoided him when the meal was over and helped Elizabeth in the kitchen.

While they were doing the dishes the mistress of Collins house confided, "Roger and the professor have never really gotten along well."

At her side drying dishes as they were passed to her, Victoria nodded. "I can tell that."

"They are such different types," Elizabeth sighed. "And Roger enjoys being nasty when he's had a few drinks."

Victoria put down a dish. "Still, the professor did go out of his way to annoy him. At least, I thought so."

Elizabeth agreed. "The professor has a strange brilliance. But he is not a pleasant man. I do believe he enjoys creating trouble. Linda, fortunately, takes after her mother."

"Did you know her mother?"

"She was a lovely girl. High strung, but from a fine family. Her tragedy was in marrying a man like the professor."

She gave the older woman a searching glance. "You seem to know him very well."

Elizabeth's cheeks showed patches of crimson. "I suppose I do. He has visited here so often."

"You don't have many such friends."

"No. The professor and his daughter are exceptions," Elizabeth said, carrying on the pretense.

When Victoria left her, she was convinced that Elizabeth would never confess the truth about her relationship to the professor. Victoria couldn't understand this. It would be so much simpler for everyone to be realistic about it. Or would it? Not if Elizabeth suspected her older brother of attempting a murder!

It was close to three o'clock when Victoria sought Linda out in the library. The dark girl was wearing an orange and black minidress that showed most of her lovely legs. She was seated in an armchair with a magazine when Victoria entered the room.

"I wondered where you were," Linda said, smiling and putting the magazine aside.

"After I helped with the dishes I took a short nap," Victoria told her. "Now I'm going over to the cottage to visit our tenant. She's an invalid and doesn't like visitors, but she does encourage me to come to see her. Yesterday I mentioned you and she suggested I bring you along as well."

Linda opened her eyes wide. "I'm flattered. To what do I owe the invitation?"

Victoria smiled. "Blame me! I'm afraid I mentioned that we were supposed to resemble each other and aroused Margaret Lucas' curiosity. She at once said she'd like to see you."

It was Linda's turn to be ashamed. "Why not?" she said rising. "Is she very ill?"

"I'd say so," Victoria told her. "She's had a serious operation which I gather was not a success. We think she had come here to die. She's very thin and pale."

"Poor woman!" Linda was genuinely sympathetic. "You'll enjoy talking to her," Victoria predicted.

As it turned out, Linda did find the woman's conversation fascinating. Margaret Lucas had tea ready for them and some delicious cakes provided by the forbidding- looking Carlos, who hovered malevolently in the background until his mistress rather curtly dismissed him.

Over the tea table Margaret Lucas knowledgeably discussed books, art and the theater with them. The girls mostly listened.

The gray-haired woman was wearing a bright crimson dressing gown that gave her some color. Victoria thought she looked much better than she had ever seen her and felt the extra company might be doing her good.

Margaret said, "I must admit I didn't believe Victoria when she said you two were supposed to look alike. But I can see the resemblance now that you're both here. I wouldn't call it marked, but there is something of the same contour and expression in each of your faces."

Linda smiled. "I think Victoria is very pretty, so I don't mind."

Victoria pointed out, "We can blame your father for starting the story."

"How long do you expect to remain at Collins House, my dear?" Margaret asked Linda.

She shrugged. "It's hard to say. I hope for a few weeks. But sometimes Dad gets a sudden notion and we're packing."

The gray-haired woman nodded. "But then, you do a great deal of traveling. You're returning to Europe when you leave here?"

"Yes. We're playing our first dates in Paris," Linda told her.

The pale woman smiled. "I know every capital of Europe. I have many friends in London and Rome. But that all seems so long ago these days." She gave a deep sigh and suddenly looked terribly weary.

Victoria was alert to her changed mood and shocked to see how tired she had become. Standing up, she hastened to say, "We mustn't stay any longer. We're overdoing it. You need to rest."

The invalid gestured wearily. "It's sad to be old and almost worn out." She studied them behind the dark glasses and with a gentle smile said, "You must come again. Both of you!"

"Thank you," Linda said. She was already on her feet.

"I enjoy having someone read to me," Margaret remarked to Linda. "Your voice has a delightful quality with that charming touch of accent. Would you care to come over mornings at eleven and read to me for an hour?"

"I'd like to," Linda said enthusiastically.

"Fine, then we'll consider it settled." The invalid hesitated, and then went on, "And now if you don't mind, my dear, I'll ask you to leave first. I have one or two things of a private nature I'd like to discuss with Victoria."

No one was more surprised than Victoria at this declaration. But Linda didn't seem to think it odd at all. She gave them both one of her charming smiles. "Of course. I'll be around at eleven tomorrow morning, Mrs. Lucas." To Victoria she added, "I'll see you at dinner."

Victoria nodded, still somewhat startled. "Yes."

As soon as Linda went out, Margaret turned to Victoria with a worried air. "Carlos told me what happened to you last night! My dear, you might have been killed!"

"I know," she said. "I was careless and I paid for it."

"Just what did take place?"

Victoria went over it briefly, realizing her friend was tired, and not wanting to tax her strength further. She finished with, "I'm almost certain it was Professor Veno."

"If you were actually pushed into the well, I can think of no one else who might have done it. Please be wary of that man."

"I intend to," Victoria said. "And now I must go."

Margaret patted her arm and kissed her on the cheek. "I'm depending on you to be sensible," she said, in parting. "Remember, I can't afford to lose you. I have no other friends."

Victoria smiled. "Now you'll have Linda."

The older woman nodded. "Yes, Linda. She is a nice little creature. But not like you, my dear."

Victoria left the cottage feeling better. Being with the invalid always cheered her. She valued Margaret Lucas' interest and friendship. And she was glad the sick woman had liked Linda. It would do her good to have an extra visitor.

Later, Victoria could ask herself why. But at the moment she walked straight past the house to the path that followed the cliff without giving it a thought. It was a pleasant afternoon and she was enjoying the air and sunshine. She strolled along the path, the breeze ruffling her long black hair, and at last she found herself standing on that high point of the cliffs Professor Veno had mentioned at dinner—the suicide spot.

Suddenly conscious of where she had strayed, she gazed down at the angry surf and the jagged rocks a hundred or more feet below and felt her heart pound fiercely. And then she heard footsteps in the gravel beside her. She turned; it was Professor Veno standing there. He doffed his wide-brimmed black hat and smiled at her. The burning, deep-set eyes fixed directly on hers.

He said, "I didn't expect to find you here, Miss Winters."

"I didn't plan to come here," she said, with a slight quaver. She tried to look away, to break the meeting of their eyes, but she couldn't.

He was speaking in a low voice. "Think of what those

other poor souls must have felt when they stood here during the last moments of their lives! Try and feel what they felt! You are desperate and about to throw yourself over the cliff. Miss Winters!" He went on monotonously, his eyes burning more wickedly than ever.

"No!" she protested. But she wasn't able to move or resist staring back into those bright, all-consuming eyes. She thought, "He is hypnotizing me. He is going to make me kill myself!" But she couldn't look away.

He came a step closer, the eyes never wavering. "You want to die! It will be so easy!"

CHAPTER 5

Victoria stood there unable to move or speak. Those weird, glittering eyes had enlarged to become her whole world. There was no escape from them. She heard the restless wash of the waves far below and she felt a great melancholy surge through her. She knew what was happening and yet she could do nothing about it. Gradually she was falling under the hypnotic spell he was so skillfully weaving. Would these terrible moments end with her hurling herself over the cliff as the others had?

"You are sad," the professor droned on, his eyes never wavering. "You are ready to say goodbye to life! And release is at hand! An easy release!"

The words he uttered so softly seemed gradually to become her own thoughts. She tried to close her eyes and break the spell, shut out those tempting, mad words, but it was no use! She merely stood there and stared back at him in a dazed, terrified way.

And then the miracle she had been waiting for and praying for happened. As if from a distance came the sound of an approaching car and the welcome intrusion served to snap her out of the spell. She looked away from the gaunt face of the professor and saw a white convertible—Burke Devlin's—approaching. He had chosen to leave the road and drive across the level grassy lawn so that now the car was only about forty feet away from them.

Professor Veno showed an expression of defeat on his sallow face. He scowled at the approaching car. "What have we here?"

Victoria was giving all her attention to the convertible and now she went forward to meet it, saying, "It's Burke Devlin!"

Burke brought the car to a halt and got out smiling. "I hope Elizabeth won't be too upset about my driving across the lawn. It seemed the easiest way to reach you and it's so very even."

"She won't mind!" Victoria assured him with a relieved smile. "Cars do drive up this far. And you came just when I needed you."

The millionaire's handsome face showed interest. "Did I?" He looked past her to where the professor was still standing. "I saw you weren't alone. It struck me you two were having some kind of serious talk."

"It was awful," she confessed in a low voice. "I'll tell you about it later." She stopped then because the professor was coming over to them.

Burke spoke first, thrusting out his hand as he greeted the man in black, "Here for a visit, Mark?"

The gaunt face still wore a disappointed expression. "Yes. Nice to see you, Burke." He extended a limp hand.

"You know Miss Winters?" Burke said.

The professor glanced at her with a forced smile. "Indeed I do. Just now we were having a most interesting conversation. Discussing the suicides who had thrown themselves from the point here and trying to imagine what they might have been thinking."

Burke glanced at her with raised eyebrows. "It sounds like a rather somber discussion to me."

She gave him a steady look. "It was the professor who did all the talking. I found myself merely a fascinated listener."

Mark Veno smiled at her malevolently. "You give me too much credit. Let me assure you it was having you here that inspired me to go into the matter in detail."

Burke Devlin seemed to be catching the overtones of their talk. His eyes narrowed slightly. "But then, you always did have a taste for the macabre, Mark. I suppose that is why you have gone so far with your magic act."

"It's not a magic act!" the professor protested with annoyance. "All my effects are of a mental nature. I deal entirely with sorcery of the mind."

"And what a challenge it must be to a man of your talents," Burke said wryly. "Do you mind if I steal Miss Winters away for a little?"

"Not at all," the professor said. Turning to her, he added, "We must continue our discussion some other time."

"Yes," she said, without enthusiasm.

Professor Veno stood there outlined against the cliff and the ocean beyond with a defeated expression on his bony features. He made no move to leave as Burke helped her into the convertible and got behind the wheel himself. And when they turned and drove back to the roadway he was still standing there motionless, sinister.

Victoria gave a great sigh and settled back against the car seat. "I think I might have been killed just now if you hadn't come when you did."

Burke glanced at her from the wheel with an inquiring frown. "What are you talking about?"

Quickly she began to tell him. He brought the convertible to a halt in the driveway in front of the house. Until she had come to the end of her story he said nothing.

Then he told her, "Mark is undoubtedly an accomplished hypnotist. You must avoid getting yourself into a situation like that again."

Her pretty face was shadowed as she asked him, "But why should he want to harm me? Unless he has some reason we aren't aware of."

Burke Devlin gave her a reproving glance. "I know what's on your mind again. You're dramatizing yourself in the role of the unwanted child. You're thinking that Mark recognizes you as the child he tried to rid himself of years ago and is attempting to do the job properly now. It's ridiculous! For one thing, all the facts indicate the child in question died at birth."

"That's what we think. But it doesn't have to be the truth. There has to be some motive for his trying to kill me."

Burke frowned. "Would it be too simple an explanation to conclude that he is mad? He might be willing to kill without a motive, or for some reason that wouldn't make sense."

Victoria gave this thoughtful consideration. "Linda said her father had many strange obsessions, that he isn't normal."

"And if his own daughter says that, you can be pretty sure it's true."

"She also spoke of his dwelling on the fact she and I look alike."

"It's hard to say what is going on in his mind," Burke warned her. "You know he has been rather odd since his youth."

"I still think it may have something to do with my parentage," she persisted. The idea that Mark Collins could be her father was repulsive to her, yet she was forced to face it as a possibility.

Burke said with annoyance, "There's not much use my arguing with you about it. You have your own obsessions. And I've known you long enough to realize that anything to do with the discovery of your parents short-circuits your brain. You'll grasp at any straw in the hope of finding out who you really are."

"Does that seem so strange?" she asked, bitterly.

He reached out and took one of her hands in his own. "No," he admitted. "But you go to extremes, just as you're doing now. Try to keep your suspicions on a logical level."

"Thanks for the advice."

He sighed and squeezed her hand. "Don't bother telling me. I know you won't follow it." He paused. "Has Elizabeth admitted to you yet who the professor really is?"

"No."

Burke withdrew his hand and looked annoyed. "I think it is about time that was settled. Before I leave, I'm going to see her. Maybe that will put an end to your being pushed into wells and hypnotized into jumping off cliffs. Mark may not be so bold if he finds out you know his true identity."

"If only Ernest would get here," Victoria mourned. "I need someone I can depend on. I tried to get you on the phone earlier to tell you about last night. I couldn't reach you. What decided you to drive over?"

He smiled. "The operator recognized your voice. I called back, thinking it must be something serious. When I couldn't reach you by phone I decided I'd try in person."

"How lucky it was you did."

He said, "I'm going to talk to Elizabeth about Mark. I'd just as soon you weren't around. Do you mind?"

She shook her head. "No. I'll go stroll in the garden for a little."

"Fine. I won't be staying here more than five or ten minutes," he promised. "And if anything happens to upset you again, don't hesitate to let me know."

"I won't," she said.

Burke left the car and went to the front door as Victoria walked in the direction of the rose garden. There she found Linda, also strolling among the flower beds and rose bushes. The girl smiled at her from under her broad-brimmed straw hat.

"Who is the handsome man that brought you to the door in his car?"

Victoria blushed. "An old friend. Burke Devlin."

"Burke Devlin!" Linda echoed. "Isn't that the mystery millionaire who has come back to town?"

"Yes."

"And I thought you told me there was no excitement in Collinsport," Linda admonished her. "All the while you've been keeping that rugged male charmer for yourself."

"It wasn't my intention," Victoria said with rueful amusement.

"When do I get to meet him?" Linda wanted to know.

"It will have to be later," Victoria said. "He's leaving in a few minutes."

Linda had a twinkle in her eyes. "I don't blame you for not wanting to share him. But I do intend to meet him."

"You will," she promised. "We can see him in town some evening."

"Not likely," Linda said. "You forget that Ernest is due here soon. And I'll be giving all my time to him."

"Yes, I had forgotten about that," Victoria said quietly. All her old doubts and worries returned.

"The garden is still quite nice," Linda said, changing the subject as she glanced around at the late-blooming flowers. "And it is past the main season. As I remember, there used to be a lot more garden."

"There was. But Matt Morgan claims he doesn't have the time to look after a bigger garden."

"That Matt!" Linda said with disgust. "He's always complaining about something or other."

They continued discussing the garden and soon she heard Burke drive away. She stayed with Linda only a few minutes longer and then made an excuse to go inside. She wondered what Burke had said to Elizabeth and was anxious to get her reaction. When she entered the front door there was no one in the hallway. But as she started upstairs Elizabeth suddenly came out of the living room. "Victoria!" the older woman called up to her.

She paused and turned on the stairway. "Yes?"

"Will you come down a minute?" Elizabeth asked, her attractive face pale and determined.

Victoria knew what she would want to discuss but wasn't sure just how Elizabeth would go about introducing the subject. When she reached the last step, she stood there waiting for her to begin.

Elizabeth looked embarrassed. "Burke has been talking to me," she said. "He explained that you know the professor is really my brother, Mark Collins."

"Yes. Burke told me the other night."

Elizabeth gave her a reproachful look. "I wish you had let me know at once."

"I didn't think it my place to say anything."

"I know you must find the situation here strange," Elizabeth went on with a sigh. "But Mark has always been the professor to us since he began coming back for visits."

"It really makes no difference to me," Victoria told her.

"I will quietly tell him you know," Elizabeth said. "But I'll ask you to go on calling him by his professional name and acting as if he were a guest. That is the way we manage this difficult situation."

"I understand."

The older woman hesitated, her eyes searching Victoria's face as if trying to discover any hidden resentment. Then she said, "Burke also pointed out that you are suspicious of the professor. You think he may have had some part in your accidents."

"You know I have wondered," Victoria said.

"And I don't blame you," Elizabeth said quickly. "He is strange in his ways and he does give people a sinister impression of himself. But I do not believe my brother capable of trying to harm anyone."

"Does Burke feel the same way?"

"I'm sure that he does," the older woman said. "At least he agreed that it would be wrong for me to talk to the police about the incident of the well. He believes we should wait awhile, just as I do."

"I see," Victoria said, by no means convinced this was true.

"I do hope you'll be patient and let me work this out as I think best," Elizabeth said. Changing the subject with obvious relief, she went on, "Linda told me she made a very good impression on my tenant. She says Mrs. Lucas wants her to read to her every morning."

"Mrs. Lucas found her charming," Victoria said. Elizabeth offered her a wan smile. "I'm glad something good is happening here. Linda is a lovely girl."

"I agree."

"That's all, Victoria," the older woman said. "And please remember, I'm only trying to do what I think best."

Victoria nodded. "I'm certain of that." She turned and went back upstairs.

As she made her way to her own room she couldn't help wondering in whose best interests Elizabeth thought she was acting. Was she desperately covering up all evidence in an attempt to save the family name from further disgrace, or was she actually trying to solve the mystery by silently waiting and watching? Victoria found it hard to believe this latter course was in her favor and she greatly doubted that Burke Devlin had concurred with the strategy either.

When she went down to help Elizabeth with dinner around five-thirty, she found Roger had returned home and was standing impatiently in the doorway of the living room with a bottle in his hand.

"Did you know all the good sherry is gone?" he asked Victoria accusingly.

She paused facing him. "I hadn't noticed, Mrs. Stoddard usually looks after the wine."

"Then she does a mighty poor job of replenishing." Roger's weak, good-looking faced registered anger. "I came in here feeling exactly like a glass of sherry and find an empty bottle."

"I'll tell her," Victoria said.

"You can do better than that," Roger Collins told her. "I want you to go down to the wine cellar and get another bottle. And remember, bring the old stock. I'll give you the key." He fumbled in his pocket.

Victoria pointed out, "Mrs. Stoddard usually selects the wine."

He passed her the key. "Nothing to stop you from doing it," he said. "I'm not going to twiddle my thumbs here with a parched throat until Elizabeth finds time to bring up a bottle. Remember, the old stock is on the lower shelf to the left as you enter the wine cellar." He handed her the empty bottle. "You may as well get rid of that too!"

Victoria considered arguing with him and then decided against it. He was right when he said there was no reason why she shouldn't be able to find the wine. She had been down to the cellar many times with Elizabeth and knew where the sherry was kept.

She left Roger waiting and went along the corridor to the cellar door. Then she switched on the light and started down the narrow stairs. The lights in the cellar reflected the inadequate, old-fashioned wiring in that part of the old mansion and were small and dim. Most of the tiny bulbs were only twenty-five watts and in the pitch-black of the cellar area they gave off only a token dim glow that dispelled utter darkness but created an eerie, shadowed atmosphere.

The cellar floor was earthen except for the tiny area where the new furnace had been installed on a concrete base. And the underground section of the house smelled damp and musty as a result. Her elongated shadow followed her down the corridor that led to the wine cellar. Though she had been down there many times with Elizabeth, she rarely ventured in the lonely region by herself. Part of the mansion was shut off and so was the cellar portion of it.

She passed the yawning dark entrance to the deserted section and her nostrils were again assaulted by an odor of decay and dampness even stronger than in the main cellar. Ahead was the padlocked wooden door leading to the wine cellar. She put down the empty bottle beside several others that had been sitting there gathering dust. Feeling a little nervous, she fumbled trying to get the key in the lock. Finally she got the padlock off and swung the door open. The pungent odor of spirits mingled with the other cellar smells. She stepped inside the wine cellar with its many rows of shelves, most of them filled with dusty bottles. As she recalled, the light was near the doorway, a drop light with a single bulb hanging from the ceiling and a snap switch on it above the bulb itself. She fumbled in the darkness until at last her hand made contact with the glass bulb and then her fingers found the switch.

She turned it, but the bulb didn't light. She tried again, still with no results. Deciding the bulb had burned out, she made up her mind to find a bottle of the good sherry in the darkness. She knew exactly where it should be and groped along the lower shelves until her fingers closed on one of the dust-coated bottles. She was about to take it to the door and check its label when the lights in the main cellar outside suddenly flicked out.

Although she had been nervous before, she hadn't known anything like real panic. But she felt it at this moment. Quickly she called out, "Mrs. Stoddard! I'm down here!" Elizabeth must have opened the cellar door, she thought, and switched the lights off, not realizing she was down there.

There was no reply to her shout. It just echoed in the empty blackness of the big cellar. She stared into the shadows, a chill going through her as she considered the long distance she had to travel before reaching the steps and the familiar region of the hall above. She stood there indecisively for a moment, her fear mounting, deciding what she must do.

She really had no choice but to start back. It was quite unlikely that whoever had turned off the lights would hear her and put them on again. Once the upstairs door had been shut she could shout forever and not be heard. With a sigh she clutched the bottle and stepped out of the wine cellar. She could not see to put the lock in place now and didn't worry about it. The door could stay open until she made the journey upstairs and managed to get the lights on again.

Still carefully holding the bottle, she edged along in the darkness. She knew she was going in the right direction and her eyes gradually became accustomed to the shadows. Something rustled on the floor ahead of her and she halted with a small cry of dismay. Thoughts of rats flashed through her mind. She knew Matt Morgan had caught some in the barns and didn't doubt they were in the cellars as well.

She stood there tensely, listening for some other movement, but the damp cellar was silent again. Fighting to curb her increasing fear, she slowly went on, guessing that she had gone at least a third of the distance to the stairs. The reason for the lights being out continued to bother her. Logic assured her that someone had accidentally turned them off, but suppose it had been done deliberately?

She tried to put the idea out of her mind. She was still shaken from her macabre encounter with the professor on the cliff and this, coming so soon afterward, was almost too much. She was trembling and ready to burst into hysterical sobs at any new development. Why had she been such a fool as to obey Roger's order to go down there?

And then the rustling sound came again, from the left. She guessed it would be from that other passage that gave entrance to the cellar under the deserted portion of the old mansion. She must be about even with it now. Crouching against the wall she clutched the bottle to her and listened, her eyes wide with terror.

The rustling came closer and then without warning took shape. Gleaming phosphorescently before her was the skull face the Phantom Mariner. She pressed against the wall screaming wildly as the monster took a step toward her so she could see the details of the skeleton head more clearly as well as the cowl surrounding it and the black, flowing robes of the ghost. Her nostrils were filled with an odor of death and decay.

Her mind reeled and she thought she would faint. And then the grinning skull vanished as quickly as it had appeared. The rustling sounds faded away and all was quiet and blackness again. She stood there a long moment, the last scream frozen on her lips, not knowing what to believe. Had it been a creature of her tortured imagination, something her fears had conjured up, or had she really seen the legendary ghost of Widow's Hill?

There was really no doubt in her mind. The luminous skull face had been too real. The thing had almost touched her and she had experienced the reek of its decay! With a sob she flung herself down the passage and raced through the darkness until she stumbled against the bottom of the steps. Then, still sobbing, she groped her way up the steep, narrow flight of stairs and finding the knob, flung the door open.

She gasped with relief as she stepped out in the comparative light and safety of the upper hall. And only then did she notice that through all the turmoil of her experience she had clutched the sherry bottle to her. Breathing rapidly and unevenly, she made her way down the hall to the living room.

Roger was nowhere in sight. She almost laughed in her despair.

"Oh, there you are!" It was Roger speaking. He had come up behind her from someplace else in the house.

She turned rapidly and held the bottle out for him. "Your wine!"

He took it but his eyes were fixed on her and he looked startled. "What's the matter with you?" he asked. "You've been crying and you look as if the devil had been chasing you."

"I think he has," she said, feeling weak and ill.

Roger touched her arm as if he'd expected her to faint. "You're really in a state! What went on down there?"

She swallowed hard. "The lights went out. I saw the ghost! The Phantom Mariner!"

"The what?"

"The death figure with the skull face. You remember the professor spoke about it."

"Damn the professor for dealing out such trash!" Roger said angrily.

"But I did see it!"

"You wouldn't have known about such a thing if he hadn't brought it up," the blond man protested. "The Phantom Mariner is a legend! I've lived here all my life and I've never seen such a figure!"

"I'm sorry," she said, feeling more embarrassed as her condition improved.

Roger was holding the bottle of wine and glaring at her. "You have no need to be sorry. It's that mad professor who started it all."

"I'm not all that impressionable," she said. "I did see something."

He frowned. "You say the lights went out?"

"Yes."

"Did a fuse go?"

"I don't know," she faltered.

He gave her another angry glance. "That's probably what happened and you had hysterics. We'll soon see." And he started down the corridor to the door that led to the cellar.

She followed him and arrived just in time to see him turn the lights on. He looked disappointed and gave her a sharp look. His easy explanation wasn't working out.

She said, "I knew someone must have turned them off."

Roger was turning sullen. "That doesn't mean it was done

on purpose."

"No."

"Elizabeth likely noticed them on," he said. "You better ask her. Did you lock up the wine cellar?"

"Not with the lights out."

"I'll do it now," he said. "Can't take any chances with all the people we have around. Saw that Carlos fellow lurking near the outside entrance to the cellar this afternoon. Don't like him! Can't see why Elizabeth had to rent the cottage!" Still grumbling, he vanished down the cellar steps.

Victoria took a deep breath. She was regaining control of herself fully now. But the memory of the shocking experience in the cellar was too vivid for her to dismiss it lightly. She had seen the Phantom Mariner for a second time. And she was well aware of the message of its appearance. It was a warning of death. After she'd seen it last time there had been the incident of the well. What threat to her life would she face next?

She went out to the kitchen and found Elizabeth busy at the stove. The older woman smiled at her. "I've everything almost ready. I'll just need you to help me carry some of the food in."

"I should have been here sooner," Victoria apologized. "I went down to the cellar to get Mr. Collins some sherry."

"Oh?" Elizabeth showed surprise. "I thought there was a good half-bottle still in the living room."

"It was empty."

Elizabeth looked perplexed. "Perhaps the professor had some of it."

"Did you turn the lights off in the cellar?" Victoria asked.

"No. Why?"

"Someone did when I was down there just now," she said. "I had to make my way upstairs in the dark."

The older woman frowned. "That's strange! I haven't even heard anyone in the hallway."

Victoria was going to tell her the rest of it but Elizabeth prevented her by handing her a large earthenware scallop dish. "If you'll just take that in to the sideboard," she told her.

Victoria took the still-hot dish out to the dining room and placed it on the sideboard to be served later. As she started back she came face to face with Professor Veno in the hallway.

"Roger has just informed me you had a nasty scare in the cellar. He blames me for filling your mind with phantoms," he said.

Victoria stood in the shadowed corridor, her way blocked by the thin man in black, feeling increasingly nervous. She was once more filled with the conviction she had known that other time, that the phantom she had encountered had been the professor in disguise. She murmured, "I'm sorry he bothered you about it."

The deep-set eyes burned into hers. "I'm glad he told me. As you know I'm interested in all types of spirit manifestations," he said quietly. "And of course we mustn't ignore the warning implied, must we?"

"The warning?" she repeated, staring into those frightening eyes.

"The warning of death, my dear," the professor said. "It was undoubtedly meant for you."

CHAPTER 6

Three days passed quietly. Victoria gradually began to forget what had happened and settle down to the new routine at Collinswood with the black sheep of the family, Mark Collins, and his daughter as guests. Elizabeth made no further reference to the fact the odd, gaunt man was her brother and all in the house continued to address him as "Professor."

Linda and Victoria became quite good friends. And every day Linda went over to read to Margaret Lucas. She seemed to enjoy this task and actually looked forward to it.

Meanwhile, Victoria was on edge waiting for Ernest to arrive. He was already days late and once before he had promised to come to Collinsport for a vacation and at the last moment he had to cancel it.

She fervently hoped this wouldn't happen this time. She wanted to see how he reacted to Linda being there and find out if there was any real romance between the two. She also hoped to discover if Ernest was likely to propose to her. Until she'd heard about his friendship with Linda she'd been almost certain he would. Now she didn't know!

Victoria made it a point to follow Burke Devlin's advice and avoid the professor as much as possible. After her close call with him at the cliff's edge she was aware of the danger he presented. She still clung to her belief that this man of mystery might be the father she had never known. She intended to follow this up after Ernest arrived, but for the moment it could wait.

Professor Veno had seemed strangely restless in the last day or two. She was almost ready to accept Burke Devlin's theory that the mentalist was insane. The glittering, deep-set eyes, the odd, somber manner of dressing, his tendency to ramble about phantoms and death—were all unhealthy signs. And there was a furtiveness in his manner as he slunk silently about the old mansion that suggested an unbalanced mind.

The other person on the estate who upset her was the hunchback, Carlos. Victoria suddenly became aware that he often followed her when she went out for a stroll, especially if she happened to be alone. She would look behind her and glimpse the stocky, twisted figure in his gray uniform, either watching her from a long distance away or pretending to be occupied with some task that kept him near where she was.

On this particular evening in late September the fog had come in heavily about seven o'clock. Feeling the need for some exercise and air before settling down for the night, Victoria decided to go as far as the cliff path. She had made sure that Professor Veno was busily occupied in an argument with Roger in the library before she started out for her walk in the mist.

Dusk was settling and it was cool. She stuffed her hands in the pockets of her blue trench coat as she stood on the path staring out toward the water. From far below she could hear the wash of waves on the rocky beach and the monotonous clanking of a buoy alternated with the hoarse note of a distant foghorn. It was the kind of night when visibility was limited to a matter of a few feet and the stage was set for phantoms. Her eyes peered into the foggy haze as she tried to make out the distant light on Rocky Head, but it was impossible to see it under these conditions.

All at once she sensed rather than heard another presence and turned to see the twisted figure of Carlos shuffle out of the mist towards her. She felt frightened and angry.

"Why do you continually follow me?" she demanded.

Carlos' grotesquely ugly face took on a sneering smile. "You make a big mistake."

"No. I've noticed. Whenever I leave the house you show up."

"You got some crazy idea," Carlos said in his heavily accented voice. "I mind my own business."

She was still angry at this new intrusion. "I'll tell Mrs. Lucas!" she threatened.

His gargoyle face took on an expression of rage. "You a smart girl, you keep your mouth shut!" he snarled.

"I won't have you following me all the time."

"Maybe you'd rather meet the ghost," the hunchback said.

She stared at him. "What do you mean by that?"

He chuckled evilly. "Is it not a good night for phantoms?"

Sharply Victoria asked, "What do you know about phantoms?"

Carlos grinned at her impudently. "Now you want to talk to me?"

"I want you to answer my question."

He spread his hands in a gesture of appeal. "What does any man know about such things?"

"I don't want your pretending," she told him angrily. "You meant something by what you said and I'm asking you to explain."

"And if I cannot?"

"Then I'll be sure you have something to conceal."

Carlos chuckled again. "You have a great deal of imagination. First you say I follow you. Then you say I hide something from you. All I do is take a walk for my health."

"Very well," she said. "But don't think you're going to get away with this. I will tell Mrs. Lucas as I warned you."

He shrugged. "That is your decision." And with that he turned and walked away, vanishing quickly in the fog.

She watched until he was out of sight. But even then she had the conviction he wasn't far away, that he was somewhere just beyond the curtain of fog, lingering to follow her when she moved on. It was unnerving! She made up her mind to mention it to Margaret Lucas when she saw her the following day, although she normally made it a rule to say nothing that might upset the sick woman.

The fog lasted all night and was still thick the following day. This was not unusual along the coast of Maine at this season of the year. Victoria rarely visited the cottage in the mornings now, since this was when Linda went over to read to the invalid. But as soon as lunch was over she changed into a dark blue wool dress suitable for the afternoon and headed for the cottage.

Carlos was nowhere in sight and Margaret herself let Victoria in. The sick woman was wearing another attractive dressing gown, a brown velvet one this time, and looked quite well. Despite the dimness of the day, she wore her customary dark glasses.

"Carlos has gone to the village to do some errands," she explained as they sat down in the living room of the cottage.

Victoria leaned forward in the chair across from her and said, "I'm glad. I wanted to speak to you about him."

"Really?"

"Yes. I hate to say this, but lately he has been following me."

"Following you?" Margaret sounded incredulous.

"There's no question of it. Particularly in the evening. Wherever I go, I find him not far away."

Margaret looked thunderstruck. "You sound as if there's no doubt about this."

"It's true, I promise you."

"But Carlos has never caused trouble of this sort before." The older woman hesitated. Then she said, "Forgive me for suggesting this. But could it be you've encouraged him in any way? I mean innocently, without meaning to?"

"I can't imagine that I have. I've barely spoken to him."

"Carlos is a lonely, unhappy man. I have tried to be good to him," the invalid went on in a distressed manner. "I can't believe he would repay me in this fashion."

Seeing how upset the sick woman was becoming, Victoria began to regret ever having mentioned the matter. She said, "Please don't let it worry you."

"But it does! I shall speak to him when he returns!"

"Perhaps if you gave him a hint," Victoria suggested. "I mean, let him know you suspect, without hurting his pride by coming right out with it. He might take it as a warning and not bother me anymore."

The gray-haired woman nodded. "I'll handle it tactfully in my own way. I understand him. If he follows you, he may be doing the same with poor Linda."

"I don't think so," she said. "She hasn't spoken about it."

"She might not notice as quickly as you," Margaret pointed out. "And I wouldn't want her to be upset in any way. I've grown very fond of her."

"Linda is a nice girl."

Margaret Lucas stared at her from behind the dark glasses. "I know what you're thinking: in spite of her father. And I fully agree. I have drawn her out a good deal during our reading sessions and I know she has had an unhappy life with that man."

"He loves her, but he is mentally unfit to be a proper parent," Victoria said.

The invalid smiled. "And this is the man who performs before the public as a celebrated mentalist! Ironic! Have you had any more trouble with him, my dear?"

"Not since that day on the cliff. And then that meeting with the Phantom Mariner in the cellar. I think it was probably him."

"It could have been," Margaret Lucas agreed. "You must continue to protect yourself from him."

"I have been more careful."

"You don't know how I worry about you," the sick woman told her. "And I'm doubly upset to find out that my Carlos has caused you annoyance. I promise that will be straightened out."

"Don't make too much of it!" Victoria begged, already

conscience-stricken that she'd unduly upset her friend. "I just wanted you to know."

"And you were quite right, my dear," Margaret said, "Now, if you'll put some hot water on, we'll have our tea."

The fog lifted about five o'clock and by six there was bright sunshine. It was a happy omen, for a few minutes after six one of the village taxis pulled up at the door and Ernest Collins emerged from it. Victoria had seen the taxi come up the gravel driveway and thinking it could be the young violinist, she'd eagerly hurried to open the front door. She was standing there smiling when he appeared.

His sensitive, handsome face wore a delighted smile as he hurried forward to take her in his arms. "It's wonderful to be home again!" he exclaimed, and then he kissed her.

It was a kiss she'd waited long for and so she let it last just a few seconds more than might be considered proper. The cab driver was standing by with Ernest's bags, smiling his approval.

Her face flaming with embarrassment, Victoria told Ernest, "You'd better not keep the man waiting, dear."

Ernest was reluctant to let her go. His tanned face showed an expression of adoration and he continued to hold her loosely by the arms. "He doesn't mind."

"Never was one to object to a little lovemaking," the driver confided.

Ernest passed him a bill. "Will that cover it?"

The driver looked delighted. He stuffed the bill in his pocket and tipped his cap. "You bet!" And he strode back to his cab to drive away.

Ernest picked up his two slim bags and they went into the house. "My plane was held up by fog," he told her. "I was afraid I'd lose more time. But I finally landed in Bangor this afternoon."

Victoria closed the door. "We've all been waiting. Did you know Professor Mark Veno and Linda are here?"

The young violinist showed slight surprise. "I guess they did mention it. That's fine. I'll be glad to see them again. Linda is a lot of fun."

Victoria thought she saw friendliness in his manner, but no hint of a man in love. She began to feel easier at once. She said, "She's been looking forward to your coming. She never tires talking of the good times you two had together in Spain."

He laughed lightly. "I think it is always that way when expatriates meet. How are Elizabeth and Roger?"

"Both well," she assured him. "You'll see them soon."

"I think I'll go right up and wash," Ernest said, moving to the foot of the stairs. "Do I have the same room?"

She nodded happily. "It's been waiting for you for days."

"And I've been waiting for it," he said, and went on upstairs with his bags.

He was hardly out of sight when the front door opened and Professor Veno entered. As he removed his broad- brimmed black hat he asked, "Wasn't that Ernest just came up in the taxi?"

"Yes," she said contentedly. "He's finally here."

Mark Veno glanced up the stairs. "Well, how fortunate. Linda will be thrilled. Does she know it yet?"

"She hasn't come down from her room."

The man in black gave her a wise look. "I doubt if she'll eat much dinner tonight. You know how it is with young lovers."

"I'm not sure that I do," she said shortly, feeling more annoyed than perhaps the situation warranted. But then, she mistrusted the professor generally. "I must go out and help Elizabeth with dinner or none of us will be eating." With this excuse, she hurriedly left him.

The kitchen was empty but a moment later Elizabeth came in from the rear hall with a basket of eggs in her hand. "Matt is getting lazier than ever," she complained.

"I've had to wait for these eggs. He never bothers with the hens unless I speak to him."

Victoria told her the news. "Ernest is upstairs unpacking. He looks grand."

"When did he arrive?" Elizabeth was all excitement.

"Just now," she said.

"Well, this is going to be a big evening," Elizabeth said with a look of pleasure on her maturely beautiful face. And with a wistful glance Victoria's way, she added, "I don't have to tell you Ernest is my favorite of all the family."

That was how it seemed with everyone. Even Roger drank a toast to Ernest's good health and success and managed to get through dinner without once fighting with anyone. Linda was ecstatic from the moment she came rushing down the stairs to kiss Ernest (Victoria thought he looked somewhat surprised) to their gathering in the living room when she took possession of the place next to him on the divan, leaving Victoria a lonesome place to herself.

While Victoria was a little shaken by the girl's behavior, she found some comfort in the fact that Ernest was more polite than enthusiastic in returning Linda's attentions. Once he caught Victoria's eye with a pleading expression on his sensitive face. So it came as a surprise when Linda suggested that he and she take a walk and he rather meekly accepted the invitation. Victoria was left in the living room with the older members of the family.

Roger looked disgruntled for the first time all evening. "Seems as if you're being left on your own," he told Victoria bluntly.

She forced a smile. "I'm sure Linda wants to talk to Ernest

about Spain."

"I'd think he'd want to talk to you about things nearer home," was Roger's comment.

Professor Veno had been standing at the window, watching his daughter and Ernest stroll off. Now he turned to the others to say, "Don't be surprised if there's a match in the making out there."

"I find your sentimental drivel revolting," Roger snapped. "Do you want to keep your mouth shut and have a game of cribbage?"

The professor rubbed a bony hand over the few strands of black hair plastered across his bald dome and said, "I'm in such good humor tonight I don't even mind doing that."

When the two men had left the living room Elizabeth gave her a glance and a faint smile. The mistress of Collinwood was wearing black velvet and white pearls and looking extremely regal.

She said, "It seems we're to be left alone. Doesn't Ernest look well?"

"Very well."

"A lot of that is thanks to you," Elizabeth told her. "You helped to bring him peace of mind after all the tragedy he knew here."

"I wonder," she said. "Could it be a new romance that has made such a change in him?"

Elizabeth raised her eyebrows. "Linda? She's just a child! Ernest couldn't be serious about her."

"I'm beginning to wonder," Victoria admitted frankly and went to the window. Ernest and Linda were no longer in sight. "She certainly is in love with him. She's not even trying to hide it."

Elizabeth sighed. "I blame Ernest for that. He should have told her about you."

"But what is there to tell?" Victoria asked pointedly. And it was true. She had no official status in Ernest's life. There was no engagement ring, nor had any definite plans been made.

"Ernest told me he loved you," the older woman said quietly. "I think that is good enough."

"Men have been known to change their minds. Especially when there is no binding agreement."

"Not Ernest!"

"Even Ernest," Victoria said with a wry smile. "I won't blame him if he's discovered that it's really Linda he loves."

Elizabeth got up and quickly moved across the room to her, her lovely face showing concern. "I don't like to hear that hurt note in your voice," she said. "You mustn't let yourself be bitter about this. I'm sure it will be alright."

Victoria shrugged. "The professor seems to have them already married."

Elizabeth's expression became grim. "You know Mark is

unstable. He is poor Linda's worst enemy."

"Yet he regards himself as a model father."

"Part of his great ego," the older woman said. "That was always his trouble. Don't listen to anything he says."

Victoria tried to sound casual. "You're probably right. I'm making a lot out of nothing." She paused. "But I do have a headache. I'm going up to my room."

"I wish you wouldn't," Elizabeth said. "Can't we stay here and talk?"

"I'd like to," she said. "It's just—I honestly don't feel well!" She hurried out of the room and upstairs in time to hide the tears that had blurred her eyes.

She went into her room and bolted the door after her. Then she sat down on her bed, and pressing her face into a pillow, sobbed softly. The thing she hadn't believed possible seemed to have happened. Linda had somehow won Ernest's heart. There seemed no doubt about it. Otherwise, he would never have let himself be dragged off like that on his first evening home.

In a way she blamed herself. She had been reluctant to marry him until she had found out the truth about her parentage. She had asked him to wait and he had agreed. Now she saw that things would have been very different if she'd accepted his ring when he'd first mentioned it. She had wanted to let their romance remain on this platonic level. She had known how close she and Ernest were and the tragedy they had overcome. It didn't seem possible any other girl would mean as much to him, that any girl would understand him as she felt she did. But Linda appeared to have somehow proven all her theories wrong.

When her first rush of her tears was over with, she began to collect herself and face up to what was an unhappy situation. She certainly would not let Ernest see how much she was hurt. Nor would she hold him to old promises or that welcoming kiss he had given her when he arrived which had spoken so fully of his love. Nor would she be bitter towards Linda. The dark girl had known little enough happiness in the rigorous stage life her father had made her lead from young girlhood. Linda deserved her chance for a better future.

She was sitting on the bed in semi-darkness. Dusk had fallen since her coming to the bedroom and she'd not bothered to turn on the light. In the midst of her gradually clearing thoughts there came a soft knock on her door. "Victoria!" It was Ernest's voice.

She hesitated a moment. Then she got up and went to the door. "Yes?" she asked without opening it.

"I'd like to talk to you," he said urgently. "I came back and found you gone."

"I have a headache."

"Please," he begged. "I have a few things I must tell you."

She hesitated again. Was she feeling equal to hearing his confession of love for Linda tonight? Hadn't it been dreadful enough without exposing herself to this? On the other hand, perhaps it would be better to get it settled. So that right away she would know where they all stood and how she should conduct herself.

Quickly she dabbed at her eyes with her handkerchief and then she opened the door. "I don't want to talk long," she said.

The night light was on in the hall and she could tell by his expression that he was upset. "I won't keep you too long," he promised. "But we can't talk here. Let's at least go downstairs."

"All right," she said.

When they reached the lower hallway, the voices of Roger and the professor could be heard from the library in argument over their card game. Ernest took her hand and led her to the door. "We'll have more privacy outside," he said. "And it isn't cold."

As soon as they began strolling along the gravel walk, she said, "Well?"

He halted and faced her. "Victoria, I hurt you tonight and it was stupid of me!"

She fought hard to keep her voice expressionless. "You did nothing wrong."

"But I did! And only because I didn't want to be too obviously blunt with Linda. The poor youngster seems to have gotten a lot of false ideas."

"Are you certain they are false?"

"Of course they are!" He came close to her and took her by the arms. "You can't believe any differently! Victoria!"

She turned her head away from him. "You don't have to apologize," she said in a low voice.

"But I do have to explain," he insisted. "I tried to be nice to Linda when we met in Spain. I didn't think it would mean so much to her. She's magnified it out of all proportion."

Victoria looked at him with troubled eyes. "Linda has been a very unhappy girl. She saw some brightness in a life with you."

"Which is not what I intended," he argued. "I didn't tell her about us then because I didn't think it important to reveal our private affairs. I see now that I should have."

"So?"

"So when she asked me to go for a walk tonight I agreed because I thought it would give me a chance to make things right with her."

For the first time Victoria felt her heart lift. Some of the pain eased and in a frightened way she began to hope. She said, "What did you tell her?"

"I was frank and yet I tried to be kind. I told her I liked her a great deal, that I had enjoyed her company in Spain. But that I had made a bad mistake. I had neglected to mention the fact that I was in love with you."

"What did she say to that?"

He looked unhappy. "She seemed stunned at first. Then she became angry. Said that I had led her on."

"Do you think you are guilty of that?"

"Not intentionally," Ernest said. "I can promise you that. I tried to make her understand why I kept silent. I had only recently lost my first wife. Our love affair was a delicate subject with me."

"And did she finally believe any of it?"

"In a way."

She gave him a bitter smile. "That doesn't seem very clear to me."

"I'm trying to find the proper words," he said, sounding very strained. "I'm sure I convinced her at last. But she insisted on clinging to some vestige of her dreams."

"I see."

"She said I might be in love with you now, but somehow she'd change it. I told her that wasn't likely. She laughed, kissed me and went upstairs. She's not an easy person to manage."

Victoria sighed. "She probably is heartbroken. I'm ashamed to be part of this, Ernest."

His grip tightened on her arms as he stared into her eyes. "Ashamed to admit your love for me?"

"No. But I wish this hadn't happened. That Linda hadn't been involved and gotten so mixed up."

"It's straightened out now," Ernest said. "She'll get over it. At least we have the air cleared."

"You make it sound as if it were all settled," she said. "I wish I could be as sure."

"If it's not, I'll talk to Linda some more," he promised.

Her eyes searched his face with gentle concern. "You are telling the truth, Ernest? It is me you love and not Linda?"

"Surely you don't need to ask me that now," he said, drawing her close for a long, meaningful kiss. In the security of his arms she at last felt that it might be all right. Yet much of her earlier uneasiness remained.

They resumed their walk and talked for almost an hour. By the time they returned to the house all the lights were out except the night light in the hallway and it was evident that the cribbage game in the library had ended and the two men had gone upstairs.

Ernest paused in the shadowed hallway, holding her hand in his as he stared around. "It's a strange old house," he said. "And it's known more than its share of mystery and tragedy."

She smiled faintly. "Yet you keep coming back to it."

He nodded. "In spite of its bitter memories. I'm a Collins and this land acts as a magnet for all the family. We keep returning."

"So it seems," she said, thinking of the errant Mark and how he also found the old mansion irresistible.

"I promised not to keep you up late," he whispered. "Well, it was in a good cause." He squeezed her hand and they started upstairs together.

Ernest saw her to the door of her room and kissed her goodnight again before going on to his own room. She went inside feeling happier than she thought possible and began to change quickly for bed. She was in her nightgown when the soft knock came on the door.

"Victoria!" It was Roger's voice, sounding low and oddly urgent.

She went over and listened. "Yes?"

"Victoria!" Her name was repeated.

"What is it?" she asked, somewhat impatiently.

Again Roger spoke her name, "Victoria!"

Hastily she donned her robe and slid the bolt back. But when she went out into the dimly lighted hall, there was no sign of anyone there.

And now the voice came from the stairs leading to the upper floor—Roger's voice, speaking in that same strangled tone, "Victoria!"

With an alarmed expression crossing her attractive face, she moved slowly to the stairs and started up them. Her name was called again from the landing.

The upper landing was even darker than her own floor. There was no night light; only the light seeping up the stairwell illuminated it. Almost directly opposite the head of the stairs was an open door. And from inside that room she heard Roger call her again.

She hesitated, then called out softly, "I'm here. What do you want?"

"Victoria!" Just her name again, but sounding as if Roger might be in pain.

She took a few steps closer to the door and peered inside the room. She could see no one. Suddenly without warning, she was shoved violently forward and the door was slammed behind her. At the same time she heard the tinkle of glass breaking on the floor. She flung herself on the door, pounding it, as she became conscious of a growing acid stench all around her. She was locked in the dark room!

CHAPTER 7

Victoria tugged frantically at the doorknob. The darkened room seemed to reek with a strange pungent odor. It filled her lungs and left her gasping for breath as she went on struggling to open the door that had so suddenly been shut to imprison her. It was useless; the door was locked. Screaming for help, she groped her way across the shadows of the room.

Stumbling with hands outstretched, she at last found the window drapes and fiercely pushed them aside. The acrid gas was burning her nostrils and causing her pain with every breath. She knew that unless she managed to get some fresh air she would faint within seconds.

Not hesitating to weigh the danger, she pounded against the window glass and a pane shattered. But the rush of fresh air she'd expected did not come. To her horror she discovered the shutters were nailed in place outside the window, preventing a full flow of air. With a strangled moan of despair she finally gave way to the unknown horror that was draining her strength and slumped down to the floor.

She was barely conscious of Elizabeth's voice crying out in alarm from some distant point. It seemed like a summons coming to her in a dream. Still partly conscious, she stirred weakly on the floor and tried to make an answer. But she doubted that she could be heard. She was just too weak; the effort was too great.

The hands beneath her armpits tugged at her and seemed to drag her across a carpeted floor and some vast distance. She was vaguely aware of what was going on, but was unable to help in any way. Now the pain in her nostrils was not so apparent and her breathing was easier.

Elizabeth's anxious face peered down at her, visible in the dim light of the hallway. "Are you all right?"

Victoria's head was still supported by the older woman's arm as she lay outstretched in the hallway. She spoke in a small voice. "I think so."

"What happened?" Elizabeth wanted to know.

She touched a hand to her temple and closed her eyes for a moment as she tried to summon her thoughts. Then in a dazed voice, she said, "Roger! He came to my door and called to me."

"Roger!" Elizabeth sounded incredulous.

Opening her eyes, she stared up at the attractive older woman and nodded. "Yes. First he spoke to me just outside the door. And then his voice kept coming to me and leading me on to the room up here."

Elizabeth frowned. "The door was closed and the key turned in the lock on the outside. Are you telling me he lured you to that room and locked you in there?"

"Yes," she said weakly.

"I find that hard to believe," Elizabeth told her. "You are sure it was Roger? Did you see him?"

"No. But I distinctly heard his voice. It sounded sort of odd, but I did recognize it."

Elizabeth studied her a moment. "It could well have been someone pretending to be Roger and imitating his voice."

"Perhaps, but I don't think so."

"I happened to be in the corridor," Elizabeth explained. "I came up here to the linen closet for some fresh sheets. I heard your screams. Was it merely being trapped in that dark room that terrified you so?"

Victoria now was well enough to sit up unsupported. She shook her head. "No, there was more than that. As the door was slammed shut, someone threw something into the room. I heard it break as it fell and the room at once began to fill up with some sort of gas."

Again Elizabeth frowned. "I unlocked the door and dragged you out. I don't think I noticed it."

"It was there all the same," Victoria insisted as she allowed Elizabeth to help her to her feet. She swayed for an instant and leaned heavily against her employer for support.

"We'll get you down to your own room," Elizabeth said. "Then I'll get in touch with the others. I wonder if some of them didn't hear you as well." She bent down to retrieve the sheets which she'd apparently dropped in the excitement. Then she gave her arm to Victoria as they started downstairs.

Victoria descended slowly, her pretty face pale with shock and showing an expression of bafflement. "I wouldn't have left my room if I hadn't recognized Roger's voice," she said.

At her side the older woman sounded worried. "I'll talk to Roger about this at once. First I want to get you safely back to your own room."

Victoria gave her a troubled glance. "I'm sure whoever it was meant to kill me. That gas almost stifled me!" She shuddered at the memory of those terrible moments.

"Don't think about it now," Elizabeth cautioned her as they reached the lower landing. "I'll bring Roger to your room and we'll see what explanation he has to offer."

Victoria could tell her employer was more concerned than she wanted to admit. Elizabeth was also convinced that what had happened was part of some macabre plot. All at once Collinwood had again become a place of unknown terror for her. And she couldn't help asking herself if the legend of the Phantom Mariner was to be played out again in full. She had seen the ghost twice now. Was she really doomed by that to a violent death?

Elizabeth saw her into her room and stood by as she sat on the edge of her bed. Then the older woman said, "Will you be all right for a moment if I go and speak to Roger?"

"Yes," Victoria said, resting her hands on the bedspread for support.

"I won't be a moment longer than I can help," Elizabeth assured her. As she reached the door she turned and added, "Don't move until I get back." And she went out.

Victoria's head was still reeling from the effects of the acrid gas and she felt ill as she tried to marshal her impressions. She distinctly recalled the tinkling of broken glass in the darkness and the pungent odor assailing her nostrils immediately afterward. Someone had deliberately tossed a vial of gas in with her and slammed and locked the door. The voice had been Roger's—or, at least, had sounded like his.

Elizabeth had seemed to think she'd been the victim of a deception, that someone had cleverly imitated Roger's voice to lead her into danger. And this at once brought thoughts of Professor Mark Veno to mind. No doubt he had dabbled in ventriloquism and the imitation of voices along with his other stage skills. If someone had impersonated Roger, certainly, the professor would be the logical suspect.

Not that it couldn't have been Roger himself, or even Ernest. This thought brought her new concern, which she quickly dismissed. Ernest had only a short time ago repeated his love for her. There could be no question of his wanting to harm her. Yet he had thoughtlessly involved himself with Linda and this had in turn created an uneasy situation in the old house. She realized she was still trembling a little and bent her head as she waited for Elizabeth's return.

She came in a few minutes with an irate, dressing-gown clad Roger at her side. He ran a hand through his rumpled blond hair and stood before Victoria with an expression of angry amazement on his almost handsome face.

"What the blue blazes am I hearing now?" he demanded. "What do you mean by telling my sister I lured you out into the hall?"

"I was sure it was you," Victoria said.

"Nonsense!" Roger protested hotly. "I've been asleep in my room. Elizabeth had a hard time rousing me."

Elizabeth's attractive face showed her perplexity as she explained to the still seated Victoria, "I did have trouble waking him."

"Now tell me just what this is all about." Roger ordered her.

Haltingly, Victoria offered her recital of what had gone on from the moment she'd heard Roger's voice outside her door first until she was rescued by Elizabeth. She knew it sounded unconvincing, especially the part about the gas filling the room, but she had to offer the facts as they'd happened.

Roger heard her out with a frown and then turned to his sister, "That's the wildest story I've ever heard. Who would have the nerve to pretend to be me?"

"The voice sounded like yours," Elizabeth pointed out quietly. "Victoria admits it was muffled and strange. But that only served to make her concerned enough to follow it upstairs."

He shook his head. "And this business about the vial of gas! Utterly preposterous! I'm going up there and take a look around."

Elizabeth's stayed with Victoria while they waited for him to return. Little was said between the two women, but Victoria knew her employer was still very upset. When Roger entered the room a few minutes later he wore a triumphant look.

"Exactly as I expected," he said. "Not a sign of any broken vial on the carpet. Nor was there any acid smell in the room."

"The door has been open for quite a time since," Victoria suggested by way of explanation.

Roger showed no interest. "The only broken glass I could find was where you broke that window pane." He gave her a sharp look. "You're lucky you didn't give your wrist a bad cut when you tried that trick, young lady. My guess is you imagined you heard a voice, wandered into the room, the door blew shut and you panicked!" He sighed with disgust. "I'm going back to bed!" And he turned and strode out.

When they were alone Victoria looked up at the older woman with a hurt expression. "He doesn't believe any of it," she said.

Elizabeth sighed. "I'm sorry," she said. "Roger isn't noted for his understanding. Still, I don't think it was he who called to you."

"But everything I said did happen."

"I'm sure of one thing," the older woman said. "That door was locked on you. I had to turn the key to get in."

Victoria stared at her. "What can it mean?"

Elizabeth touched a hand to her shoulder. "I have an idea we'll know soon enough. For the time being there's nothing to be done. I suggest you try and get some sleep."

Victoria locked and bolted the door after Elizabeth had gone, but sleep proved elusive. She lay awake in the darkness for a long time trying to think it all out and when at last she did rest she dreamed of the Phantom Mariner stalking her in the shadows.

The bright sunshine of the following morning had a mocking quality to it after the night of terror she'd experienced. And when she went down to breakfast she was somewhat embarrassed to find the only one seated at the big table in the dining room was Linda.

The pretty dark girl smiled coolly and said, "We're the late ones. The others have all finished breakfast and gone their various ways."

"I intended to be down earlier," she said with a touch of awkwardness as she helped herself from the ample breakfast buffet Elizabeth had set out on the long sideboard.

Linda eyed Victoria steadily. "Did you and Ernest have a nice stroll last night?"

Victoria took a sip of her orange juice. "We didn't go far. We had a lot of talk to catch up on."

"You look pale and tired. You must have been up late." There was a taunting note in the other girl's voice that suggested she knew more about the reason for Victoria's wan appearance than she was saying. She found herself considering whether Linda and her sinister father bad devised the trap for her last night in an effort to eliminate her as a rival for Ernest's affections. Then she rejected the idea. Whatever Professor Veno might be, she felt his daughter was more his victim than a possible accomplice.

Carefully, she responded, "I didn't sleep well last night."

"Probably the excitement of Ernest returning."

"That could be part of it." ·

Linda held her coffee cup in both hands and studied her above it. "Let's not pretend," she said. "I'm sure Ernest told you about me."

"About you?"

"That I foolishly declared my love for him without considering that he might already be in love with someone else."

Victoria looked down at her half-empty glass of orange juice. Quietly she said, "I don't think I need be told anything about that."

"I insist!" Linda said with surprising sharpness as she placed her coffee cup down. "He made no secret of the fact you two were in love. You might have told me before he came and saved me some embarrassment."

"I didn't know." Their eyes met. "I mean, I wasn't sure."

Linda shrugged. "Ernest doesn't seem to have any doubts."

"We're not engaged."

"He explained that. The dismal bit about his not yet being over his wife's death," Linda said lightly. "But at the moment you're the chosen girl."

"I'm not sure Ernest knows his own mind at this time," Victoria said in an effort to make it easier for the other girl. She got up to help herself to a bowl of oatmeal from the sideboard.

"I couldn't agree with you more," Linda said while Victoria's back was still to her. When Victoria returned to the table with her cereal, Linda went on blithely, "I told Ernest I wished you both luck. And I do."

"That was very generous of you," Victoria said carefully.

Linda smiled. "Perhaps not as generous as you might think. Men are impressed by good losers. I had already lost enough stature with Ernest. I had to make the graceful gesture."

Victoria helped herself to cream. "You must know I'm sorry about this complication. I want you as my friend."

Linda sat back in her chair, the lovely eyes skeptical as they surveyed her. "And of course that's your kindly attitude in return. Don't waste any energy on it. I still mean to take Ernest from you if I can."

Victoria was forced to smile at the girl's directness. "At least you're honest."

"And determined," the other girl assured her. "I've had to be in order to survive as a person with a father like mine. When I make up my mind to have something I usually get it."

"Good for you."

"And I want Ernest."

Victoria nodded. "He told me you said something of that sort to him."

Now Linda smiled and not too pleasantly. "But Ernest didn't really believe it. He doesn't think I'm capable of mean female wiles. And he's so wrong. That's why I'm warning you again. I'm not giving up where he's concerned."

"Thanks for being so frank."

Linda studied her. "You're not worried yet. But you may be. My father set down a lot of rules for me when I was a youngster. He wouldn't even let me have a picture of my mother because he hated her so. And he forbade me ever to get in touch with her. But I managed. And he's not an easy person to deceive."

"I can believe that," Victoria said quietly.

"Up until now I've had an unhappy life," Linda went on. "I think Ernest could change all that. And I'm going to try and win him from you." She got up. "I felt we should talk this out."

"It really wasn't necessary."

"Gives me a clear conscience to go ahead," Linda said with another of her tight feline smiles. "But otherwise I see no reason why we shouldn't go on being friends."

"Nor do I," Victoria said warmly.

Linda's eyes were mocking. "Just don't underestimate me as an opponent," she said. And then she quickly left the dining room.

Victoria watched after her. The slim, sun-tanned girl in white shorts and sweater could indeed be a formidable opponent. She had charm and assurance; undoubtedly she'd already plotted her strategy to win Ernest's favor, now that she knew where she stood. And there was no doubt in Victoria's mind that Professor Veno was also eager to help his daughter win the young violinist for herself. Surely it had been he who had masqueraded as Roger last night and tried to kill her. She finished breakfast feeling unsure of herself and her future at Collinwood.

When she took her dishes out to the kitchen she met Elizabeth. The lovely mistress of the old mansion was busy at the stove and turned to greet her with a smile.

"I hope you're feeling better," she said.

Victoria stacked the dirty dishes by the sink. "I am. Although I didn't rest well."

"I'm not surprised," Elizabeth said. And then, "I looked out the side window in time to see Ernest and Linda drive off in the station wagon. He asked me if he could have it to go into the village and I imagine Linda invited herself along for the trip."

Victoria had an unhappy moment. "No doubt," she agreed dully. So Linda was already embarked on her campaign.

When shortly before eleven Linda had not returned from the

drive with Ernest, Victoria remembered that it was time for the girl to go to the cottage and read to Margaret Lucas. Because she did not want to have the pleasant invalid disappointed, Victoria decided to go see her and take Linda's place as a reader if she wished it.

When Victoria arrived at the cottage Carlos was sunning himself in a garden chair, his white shirt open at the neck. On seeing her, his gargoyle face took on the usual sour grin.

Raising himself in the chair, he inquired, "Maybe you want to complain about me being here, same as you did the other night?"

Victoria tried to curb her dislike for him. "I think you misunderstood me," she said, hesitating at the cottage door.

His eyes met hers. "You spoke to her about me," he said, indicating the cottage with a jerk of his head. "You try to cause trouble."

"You're wrong."

"You got trouble enough," Carlos told her. "You better leave me alone. And you better get away from Collinsport while you're healthy."

She frowned. "Is that a threat?"

"More like a prediction," he said with a sneering smile and then he walked off to vanish among the bushes.

She started after him and then knocked on the cottage door. After a moment Margaret Lucas opened it. Despite her colorful dressing gown, her face was deathly white behind the dark glasses. She looked to be in pain.

Victoria was at once alarmed. She said, "I'm sorry to disturb you. But I thought you might be expecting Linda."

"I was," the invalid agreed, stepping back. "Won't you come in?"

Victoria entered the neat living room of the cottage. And as Margaret closed the door, she said, "I'm afraid Linda isn't likely to get here today. She went for a drive with Ernest Collins."

The pain-stricken face of the invalid took on a faint smile. "But of course. That would be the young man she met in Spain."

Again Victoria had a moment of profound unhappiness. "Yes."

"Well," the invalid said. "I'm not one to begrudge young people pleasure! I quite understand. I'm sure those two must be delighted to see each other again." She gave Victoria a glance of understanding. "But then it is difficult for you, isn't it? I had forgotten how much you care for Ernest yourself."

Victoria tried for a brave front. "He's not bound to me in any way."

"But you do feel he loves you?"

"He says he does."

The invalid regarded her sympathetically. "Then I wouldn't worry if I were you. I'm sure he's merely being kind to the other little girl."

Victoria shrugged. "Only this morning she told me she means to take him from me if she can."

Margaret Lucas sighed. "I wouldn't let that upset you. I've grown to know Linda very well and I think behind that cold veneer she's actually a very kind, well-meaning girl. As an example, consider her devotion in coming here and reading to me."

"I like Linda," Victoria said. "But I'm afraid of her father."

"He must be a strange person, from what you've told me," Margaret agreed. "Do come and sit with me awhile. I haven't had a good morning." She led the way into her bedroom.

Victoria followed, saying, "I'd be glad to read to you, if you like."

The invalid waved her to an easy chair opposite her own. "That won't be necessary. Just talk to me. Tell me what has been happening to you."

So Victoria gave the sick woman a full account of the strange events of the previous night. Mrs. Lucas listened to her with a rapt expression on her pale, lined face.

When Victoria had finished, the invalid said, "I agree with you, my dear. It must have been that crafty Professor Veno who impersonated Roger and attacked you. You must be much more careful in the future."

"I plan to be," she said.

"He must be mad—as your friend, Burke Devlin, suggested."

"Or the father who deserted me years ago," Victoria said bitterly. "I haven't ruled out that possibility."

Margaret Lucas seemed touched. "You poor unhappy dear!" she exclaimed. "So much of your life is shadowed in mystery. And now your future is being threatened by Linda."

"I don't see it that way," Victoria declared. "But I do wish I knew the full truth about myself. Often I'm certain Elizabeth knows and won't tell me."

The invalid nodded. "Mrs. Stoddard is a strange woman. I'm sure she is capable of concealing truth if she feels she has sufficient motive."

"And the motive in this case could be protecting someone else," Victoria said.

Margaret abruptly changed the subject. "Has Carlos bothered you anymore?"

"Not really," she said.

"I gave him a lecture," the invalid assured her. "I warned him not to follow you."

"I'm sure it didn't mean anything," she said. "I must go back to the house and help Elizabeth." She rose. "Are you certain you don't want me to read to you?"

"Not this morning," Margaret said gently. "I'm having a good deal of pain and I wouldn't enjoy it anyway. But please do come back again soon."

Victoria promised that she would. She walked slowly back to Collinwood, and when she reached the rear door she paused to see if the station wagon had returned. It hadn't. So Ernest and Linda must still be in Collinsport or driving through the countryside together. She blushed, knowing that she felt a strong jealousy of the dark girl.

In spite of Ernest's protestations of love, she was aware of Linda's charm. There was a real possibility Linda might change the young violinist's mind if she worked at it hard enough. And Linda had warned her that she was determined.

Entering the kitchen, she found it deserted. This increased her bleak feelings. She had hoped that Elizabeth might still be there and she would be able to throw off some of her feeling of depression through a chat with the older woman. But there was only cold silence to greet her there.

She made her way along the corridor and saw that the door to the cellar was partly ajar but no stair light was on. It could be that Elizabeth had gone down there for something or other, although she doubted it since the light was out. And after her encounter with the Phantom Mariner in the shadowed subterranean depths, she had little desire to go down anyway. It occurred to her that perhaps Elizabeth had gone up to the bedroom area to work. As there were no servants in the house, all the work was shared jointly by herself and the older woman.

With this in mind, Victoria started upstairs. She felt increasingly nervous in the deathly quiet of the old mansion. She tried the bedrooms on the second floor, but there was no sign of Elizabeth. She went on to the third floor and searched for her there. Again she was met only by the ominous silence that seemed to have taken over the ancient house.

With a puzzled frown on her pretty face, she stood in the third floor corridor considering.

Elizabeth had probably gone to the cellar, after all. Then her eyes caught the stairs leading to the attic and the captain's walk. It was possible Elizabeth was up there. Often on a fine morning like this she treated herself to a few minutes in the cupola atop the mansion to enjoy the sunshine and view. Most of the fine houses in Maine had these towers that were known as captain's or widow's walks. The name originated from the fact that retired sea captains or their widows often had these cupolas built to remind them of their days on the bridge of some fast clipper ship.

Victoria mounted the winding, narrow stairway. The creepy silence that had disturbed her since her return from the cottage still surrounded her with a brooding, sullen pressure. She felt jittery and hoped that she would find Elizabeth above.

She passed the attic level and ascended the remaining spiral steps to the door leading to the cupola. When she at last pushed it open and stepped outside she found it deserted. But because of the warm sunshine and the great panorama spread out under the cloudless blue sky, she stood there for a moment enthralled.

She could see the small village of Collinsport clearly with the canning factory standing out prominently against the shoreline. Cars made their way along the ribbon-like paved roads, but she saw no sign of the station wagon. Far below in the garden, Matt was bent over a flower bed. The season was coming to an end, and the early frosts would quickly kill the remaining blooms. She realized that Elizabeth must have gone to the cellar, since she would certainly not leave the house.

Taking a last look around at the magnificent view, she decided to go down again and try and find her employer. But before she could move she heard the creak of a board behind her and then there was a hand on her arm. She wheeled around with a frightened cry and found herself staring into the sallow, bony face of Professor Mark Veno.

The weird, bright eyes fastened on hers and he spoke softly. "Surely, you are not afraid of me."

The surprise of his sudden appearance and the firm grip of his fingers around her arm caused a surge of fear to race through her. She stared at the malevolent face and backed quickly against the wooden railing.

In an effort to quell her panic she murmured, "No. I'm not afraid."

The too-bright eyes bored into hers. "It is so high up here," he went on. "I would think it would make you dizzy."

She shook her head, partly to break the spell of those eyes. She was not successful. She was still held by his evil glance.

"I'm not afraid of high places," she said.

The sallow face under the wide-brimmed black hat took on a sinister smile, "You should be," he said softly. "You might grow careless and have a fall." And as he spoke he moved slowly closer to her so that she was now pressed tightly against the railing.

CHAPTER 8

Once again she experienced the terror she had known on the cliff. She was certain he was trying to hypnotize her. She leaned back against the railing and tried to match her will against his.

"I was looking for Elizabeth," she said weakly.

The eyes never left hers. The pupils seemed to enlarge until they were swimming dark circles that swept her whole being into them. Her hands gripped the wooden rail so fiercely the effort hurt her and she had a sensation of dizziness. The professor's spell was taking hold of her.

"I thought you had come up to study Widow's Hill," he said in his softly controlled voice, the bright eyes never flinching as a smile creased his emaciated face. "Even on a day as lovely as this it has a tragic aspect. Can't you imagine the waiting and weeping womenfolk of the fishermen huddled on the high point of the cliffs, searching the gray horizon for some sign of a boat? Waiting and wondering who would be the bereaved this time!"

"I hadn't thought about it at all," she lied in a faltering, frightened voice.

"And how those unfortunate ones felt who saw the Phantom Mariner and knew that death was to visit them, that they were bound to lose their loved one? Surely they must have contemplated suicide? They must have shrunk back in terror, ready to hurl themselves to their deaths."

As he paused, she made another effort to free herself. "Please, I don't feel well. I want to go back downstairs."

The professor made no move. He blocked her way and kept her relentlessly against the flimsy railing that was all that separated her from the long drop to the grounds below. The malevolent smile still lingered on his sallow face. In a soft, insinuating tone, he said, "And, you too have seen the Phantom Mariner?"

She shook her head in dumb fear, so transfixed by those evil eyes she was unable to speak. Gradually she was sinking under his spell. It could only be a question of a few minutes until she would be a robot controlled by his will. With a last desperate effort she found her voice and in weak protest told him, "I don't want to talk about such things!"

"But you did see the phantom!" His tone was triumphantly mocking. He knew he was winning.

"No!"

"But we all heard about it," he insisted. "And to see the Phantom Mariner is a certain omen of death! Your death!"

"Mark!" The name was called out sharply, almost reprovingly. Elizabeth Stoddard had suddenly appeared beside them on the cupola, her expression stern.

The man in black wheeled on her angrily, at the same time freeing Victoria's arm from his cruel grip. "What are you doing up here?"

"I could very well ask you the same thing," she said, frowning. She turned solicitously to Victoria. "Are you all right, my dear? You look very pale."

Victoria glanced at her, knowing that fright was written on her face. Then she looked at the scowling, forbidding face of the professor. She said, "I have a headache. I came up here looking for you. I planned to go back down again at once."

Professor Veno smiled coldly and falsely for his sister's benefit. "Then I joined her and prevailed upon her to consider the scenery with me."

Victoria had never seen Elizabeth in such a defiant mood before. She stood there on the sun-drenched captain's walk with the breeze slightly stirring strands of her dark hair and gazed at the professor with an air of disdain.

Then Elizabeth said, "Because you have been given the privileges of this house, brother, do not think I will allow you to abuse your position."

The sallow-faced man stiffened. "We do not need to discuss our problems before strangers," he snapped.

"Victoria is no stranger," Elizabeth said with a calm reproof.

"And while she is under this roof she has my protection."

"How convenient for her," the professor said sarcastically. "I assure you I have done nothing more than try to entertain her."

Elizabeth's attractive face still showed annoyance. "I think she can do with a little less of your type of entertaining."

He shrugged. "I'm sorry." To Victoria, he added with a sour smile, "I had no idea my company was repugnant to you." With this he turned and vanished through the doorway leading to the spiral stairs.

They were left alone on the cupola. Elizabeth moved closer to Victoria and said, "I was in the cellar. I began to wonder where you were and eventually came up here." She paused. "You must be careful not to be alone with my Mark."

Victoria nodded weakly. "I had no idea he would behave so strangely."

"He is a weird, twisted person," Elizabeth went on. "Because he is our brother, Roger and I try to treat him well when he is our guest. But too often he makes it difficult for us."

"I understand," she said.

"Just keep in mind what I've told you," Elizabeth said. "Never allow yourself to be isolated in his company. And now we must go down and prepare lunch. The others will be returning."

Everyone gathered in the big dining room for lunch, which proved to be a rather difficult occasion. Linda and Ernest returned from their expedition to Collinsport only a few minutes before lunch was ready, so Victoria had had no time to speak with the young violinist privately. Linda wore a smug smile of elation and told of their pleasant drive to Ellsworth and back.

"We stopped by Carolyn's school and spoke to her a moment," she told Elizabeth, who was presiding at the head of the table.

The older woman showed interest. "I had an idea you must have found something to keep you longer than you expected."

Ernest glanced across the table at Victoria with an apologetic smile. "I'm afraid I let Linda's enthusiasm for a drive along the shore make me forget the time."

From the end of the table Professor Veno remarked with mocking approval, "It's quite understandable—two young people enjoying a romantic excursion in the country."

Victoria felt her cheeks crimson and she glanced down at her salad plate. She knew Linda had deliberately kept the young violinist away to annoy her. It was her first move in what was clearly a plan to win Ernest for herself.

Elizabeth said lightly, "I've been doing some thinking this morning. It is time this house had a little gaiety."

Roger, who had been silently and morosely busying himself with his salad up to this point, gave her an inquiring look. "What brought you to that unusual state of mind?"

Elizabeth smiled at her brother. "I know I haven't encouraged visitors here or offered any kind of hospitality in ages. But I think we should celebrate Linda's being here. And I plan to give a party in her honor."

Linda's eager, happy eyes belied her words as she protested, "You really mustn't bother, Elizabeth!"

Elizabeth shook her head. "It's no use arguing. I've decided. We're having a costume party before you leave. It will give Ernest a chance to meet some of his old friends in the area as well."

Ernest looked doubtful. "You're sure you want to go through with it?" he asked Elizabeth. "You've lived here so quietly for such a long while."

"I know," she agreed. "And I do not intend to change my ways. But for this one occasion we will have music and dancing—a party on the scale of the ones we held in the old days."

Roger glanced around the table. "It's something I never expected to hear," he said. "I'm all for it. I think this old house might be better for a lively evening."

"Of course I agree," Professor Veno said smoothly. "Especially since it is in my daughter's honor."

"When do you plan to have it, Elizabeth?" Linda asked, not bothering to hide her excitement any longer.

"The sooner the better," Elizabeth said. "It will take some preparation. And I'd like to have it on a Saturday night, so Carolyn can come home and attend. I'd say a week from this coming Saturday. That will give us ten days."

Roger nodded his approval. "Invitations will have to be sent out. And there's only you and Victoria to get the house ready, unless you bring in some extra help."

"I'll be glad to do my part of the work," Linda said.

Elizabeth smiled. "We won't worry about that now. I'll start on a list and get Victoria to write the invitations and send them as soon as possible." She glanced at Ernest. "You can let me know anyone you especially want invited."

The young violinist seemed uneasy. "There are not too many people left here whom I know that well."

"Burke Devlin, of course," Elizabeth reminded him.

"I would enjoy having Burke here," Ernest agreed.

And so lunch ended with a discussion of plans for the party. Afterward, Victoria helped Elizabeth with the dishes, leaving Linda free to devote more time to Ernest. Victoria was on edge and almost dropped one of the good salad dishes as she was drying it.

Elizabeth gave her an understanding smile.

"You've helped me enough," she said. "Why don't you take a little time to yourself and talk to Ernest?"

Victoria blushed as she picked up another dish to dry it. "I'll finish up."

Elizabeth drained the dishpan into the sink. "There are only a few things left to dry anyway," she said. "And I'd really feel better if you did go now."

Victoria hesitated. "You're sure?"

"Very sure," Elizabeth said with a motherly smile and touched her gently on the arm. "And that party I'm planning is as much for your benefit as Linda's, although I didn't say so at the table. I want you to make yourself a really stunning costume and be the belle of the ball."

Victoria was touched by the older woman's interest in her. "It will be my first big house party."

"We'll make it a good one," Elizabeth promised. "Now you run along and enjoy some of this lovely afternoon."

Victoria quickly took off her apron and checked her appearance in the kitchen mirror. Her rich tan left her little need for makeup beyond lipstick and her long dark hair was in reasonable order. She had put on a fresh cotton dress for lunch; there would be no need to change. After a last quick dab of lipstick she hurried to the front of the house. There was no one around, so she went on out the front door. Ernest was standing talking to the hired man, Matt, who was finally sawing off the stump of the tree that had come down in the storm.

Seeing her, Ernest ended his conversation with Matt and came to meet her with a pleased expression on his sensitive face. "I've been hoping you'd show up."

Victoria gave him a teasing glance. "I thought you'd be exhausted after your exciting morning with Linda."

Ernest winced. "Don't rub it in! You know that extra drive to Ellsworth was her idea."

She pretended to pout. "I don't imagine you took too much persuading."

"Come on, now," Ernest said, linking his arm in hers and heading her across the grounds toward the path leading up to Widow's Hill. "I was itching to get back all the time."

"It's a wonder she didn't stay with you," Victoria said, looking up at him in amusement. "You know she's promised to take you from me."

"That's her story," Ernest said, as they continued to stroll away from the old mansion. "I let her know I wanted to be alone. It meant explaining that, like all musicians, I had moods. I hope she believed it."

Victoria laughed. "She should, since it's true."

"I didn't expect that from you," he reproved her. "Anyway, she decided to go to the cottage and read to that sick woman. She missed her session with her this morning."

She nodded. "I went over and told Mrs. Lucas you two were away in the car."

"How long has that Lucas woman been here?"

"Almost two months."

"Sort of mysterious, isn't she?" Ernest suggested.

They were now on the path itself with the ocean and the beach on their left. "Not really," she said. "Elizabeth and I feel very sorry for her. She doesn't say much. But she was operated on, and now she's having a lot of pain again."

Ernest raised his eyebrows. "You think she's in bad shape, then?"

"I'd say she was dying."

"As I understand it, she doesn't encourage any visitors other than you and Linda," he said.

"That's about it," she agreed. "I was even surprised that she took to Linda so quickly."

"Linda says she spends most of her time reading to her," Ernest said. "And Linda does have a pleasant voice."

"She's attractive in most ways."

He whooped with laughter. "Don't be catty!" he said. "You know how I meant it. I can see that this reading might be a pleasant change for the sick woman."

"Margaret Lucas is grateful to her," Victoria admitted as they neared the high point of the cliff.

"That Carlos is an odd one. Where would she pick up a servant like that?"

"Probably in her travels. She's a very interesting person. She's been all around the world."

"So have I," he said. "And I think I'd have found myself someone more agreeable and less grotesque-looking, if I'd been in her place."

"Carlos is difficult, but he is also very devoted to her," Victoria said.

Ernest smiled. "I guess it's none of my business anyway."

They were at the point of Widow's Hill that had become known as the suicide cliff. Far below them the angry waves dashed in on the rugged, rocky shore. A gull screamed, circling in the distance, and a hint of fog had begun to show on the horizon and bring a chill of dampness to the air.

Ernest put an arm around her as they studied the ocean. "I

think I would like to come back here and live one day," he said in a quiet voice.

"In spite of all that has happened here?" She couldn't forget his first wife and the tragedy of her death.

"In spite of all that," he said. "There is something about this place that keeps drawing me back."

"It seems to be the same with the professor."

"Mark Collins? Yes. Even though he disgraced himself and had to leave and change his name and way of life, he still can't resist the old place," Ernest agreed. "And then Linda will inherit her share of the Collins fortune one day."

"Naturally he's very conscious of that," Victoria said, "since he was cut out of his father's will."

"He's never been reconciled to that. I have an idea it's the reason he comes here as much as he does. He likes to flaunt his right to do so before Elizabeth and Roger."

She gave a small shiver. "He's even more frightening than Carlos. He terrifies me."

Ernest regarded her with surprise. "Why do you say that?"

She looked up at him. "I know you won't believe it. But I think he's made several attempts to kill me."

The young violinist regarded her incredulously. "You're joking!"

"I wish I was."

He stared at her. "I know Linda's father is rather unprepossessing, but I can't think of him as a would-be killer. What possible reason could he have for wanting to harm you?"

"I'm not sure. But he could have several reasons."

"Such as?"

"He could want me eliminated as Linda's rival for your affections."

"That's absurd."

"Not to a man like Professor Veno. I think he will do anything to have his way. And I mean anything! Including murder."

"What other reason could he have?"

She hesitated. "I'm not certain. But I think it might have to do with my past. That he may know the truth about my parentage."

"Why do you say that?"

"It's possible he could be the father who deserted me. It fits in with the facts," she told him solemnly.

He gave her a worried look. "You'd do better not to delve in the past. All your previous ideas have turned out to be wild fancies. And I'd be willing to bet this new theory does as well."

"Perhaps so," she said, unconvinced. "But Elizabeth has

warned me against being alone with him."

"Elizabeth said that?"

"Yes."

"Did she explain why?" The handsome face of the violinist showed fresh concern.

Apparently her mention of Elizabeth's warning had made him give her fears new consideration.

"She didn't go into any details," Victoria said. "But I'm sure she knows more than she's telling me."

Ernest frowned and glanced out at the ocean. "The fog is coming in fast."

She took it as a hint he didn't want to pursue the subject any further. She said, "Probably by five o'clock it will be really heavy."

He turned to her again, still looking worried. "I think so," he said. "How do you feel about Elizabeth's party idea?"

"Surprised."

"So was I," he admitted. "Still, it might be good for her. Good for us all. I have an idea we're getting morbid."

Victoria smiled. "You think one night of festivity will change the character of Collinwood? There'll be no more secrets or ghosts?"

He joined her smile with one of his own. "Hardly. But let us say it could be a step in the right direction."

She sighed. "I'll admit I'm looking forward to it already. And I'm also beginning to feel sad."

"About what?"

"Two days have gone by and before I know it you'll be leaving again," she said, her dark eyes meeting his.

He took her in his arms. "I'll be here for a long while yet."

"Not really."

"I may be able to stay longer than I planned," he promised. "The tour dates are not quite settled and I'm working on an original concerto while I'm here, so my time won't be wasted."

Victoria was impressed. "I didn't know."

Still holding her in his arms, he smiled at her. "I was saving it for a surprise. It's the first important composition I've attempted. If it goes well I'm going to include it in my new concerts."

"I'd love to hear you play before a concert audience," she said. "I never have."

"One day you'll be with me whenever I play," he promised her, a new light of gentleness in his eyes. And he drew her close to him for a long and ardent kiss.

After a moment she pulled herself away and stared up into his handsome face with a rueful smile. "We'll be talked about. They can still see us from the house."

"I don't care!"

"What about Linda?"

"Better that she see us. She'll be more ready to give up any false hopes."

Victoria sighed. "I don't want to make her unhappy. She hasn't had an easy life with that father of hers."

He raised his eyebrows. "Don't tell me you're pleading her case!"

"No, but I do think she's gone through a lot," Victoria insisted. "Never knowing her mother, and the professor making her work in his mental act with him from the time she left boarding school. She's never known a proper home or girlhood."

"I agree with you," he said. "But she's a difficult person. She has inherited some of her father's hardness and erratic nature."

"That could be true. But he's the one I'm afraid of."

Ernest frowned. "You were really serious about that?"

"It seems almost certain it had to be him."

"Have you any proof?"

"No. But things have happened. Things that have no reasonable explanation. In every case the evidence has pointed to the professor."

"You've discussed this with Elizabeth?"

"Several times. At first she put me off. But today she warned me. I'm sure she believes as I do that the professor is trying to place me under a hypnotic spell."

Ernest studied her with a worried expression. "I think I should talk this over with her."

"No. It wouldn't do any good. And I'll be more cautious from now on."

"But I don't want you in danger!"

She offered him a faint smile. "I'm not sure that I am," she reminded him. "I promise to tell you if anything else happens."

"I'll depend on that," he said.

Arm in arm they began to walk back toward the old mansion with its many chimneys and the crowning captain's walk. The fog had moved in a bit more to give that afternoon a mournful touch. The bright sun was obscured and there was a new coldness in the air.

"It doesn't look as if it would be a very nice evening," Ernest observed. "I think I'll shut myself in my room and work on the concerto."

"Probably it would be a good time to do it," Victoria agreed, although she regretted that she would lose his company.

He gave her a frowning glance. "I'd watch that Carlos," he warned. "It could be that some of your trouble comes from that direction."

"Please don't let it bother you," she protested, almost sorry that she had confided in him.

"You can't expect me not to worry some," he said.

"I can hardly wait for the party," Victoria said, changing the subject deliberately. "It will be wonderful to see the old house really alive."

"Yes," he agreed moodily, "the party is a good idea." But she could tell that he was still worrying about what she had told him.

After dinner Ernest at once excused himself and went upstairs to work on his concerto. The others gathered by the fireplace in the big living room and Roger started a log fire. The fog had now really settled heavily over all the area, making it damp and uncomfortable. Professor Veno stood at one side of the fireplace, his sallow face brooding as he stared into the swirling red and yellow flames. The flickering blaze reflected on the bony face of the black-garbed man made him look more Satanic than ever.

Even with the others there, Victoria felt uneasy in his presence. Linda was in an exuberant mood as she discussed the proposed party with Elizabeth. Victoria felt left out of it and longed for Ernest to be there. At last Roger led the professor off to the study for one of their games of cribbage and Linda excused herself to go up to her room and write some letters.

As she rose she gave Victoria an arch smile. "So Ernest is working tonight."

"Yes," Victoria said.

"Too bad," Linda said without conviction. "But then, he did have some fun this morning, so I suppose he feels he should take some time to work." And with a tormenting smile she turned and went out.

Elizabeth, seated in an easy chair by the fireplace, glanced at Victoria with an amused expression after her niece had left. "You mustn't be too sensitive, my dear," she said. "I'm sure you have nothing to worry about."

Victoria didn't feel like discussing the rivalry between herself and Linda for Ernest's affections. Flushing a little, she asked, "Do you mind if I drive into town for a half-hour?"

Elizabeth hesitated. "It's not a good night for driving. It's very foggy."

"But I know the road so well," Victoria said. "And I do feel I want to get away from the house for a while."

Elizabeth looked reluctant but she said, "If you're sure you'll be all right, and promise not to stay in Collinsport late."

Victoria was already on her feet. "I promise." At once she started out of the room before her employer could have any second thoughts on the matter.

She put on a scarf and sweater to protect herself against the cold fog. The night had darkened prematurely because of the heavy mist and as she took her place behind the wheel of the station wagon she realized Elizabeth had been right. It was one of those truly difficult nights to drive, with the kind of heavy fog found only in coastal Maine.

She was going to see Burke Devlin. She had not phoned in advance as she usually did, but he was in Collinsport most of the time. On his few excursions to Boston or New York he generally called to let her know he would be away. And he had told her to keep him in touch with her problems at Collinwood.

Certainly she had plenty to tell him. He would be interested in the party which Elizabeth was planning. He would be among those invited. She headed the car toward the woods road and the strong headlights only cut the fog for a few feet. She would have to go slowly.

The eerie, swirling night mists began to have their effect on her nerves. This was surely a night for phantoms. Her thoughts turned to the legendary Phantom Mariner. The remembrance of the spectral cowled figure with its grinning skeleton face was burned in her mind. She frowned and again tried to convince herself that it had been Professor Veno in the disguise of the phantom trying to terrify her and make her a more compliant victim to his will.

Those burning eyes had more than once threatened her. Earlier in the day she had known her worst moment with him. Alone with him on the captain's walk she had felt certain she was falling under the spell of his weird eyes. And once she was under his power he could easily have persuaded her to hurl herself over the cupola's railing.

The trees seemed to close in on either side of the road, their branches reaching out like arms. Before her, the headlights created only a misty blur.

And then from out of the darkness a strange apparition was outlined in the glare of the headlights—a grotesquely ugly face and arms waving in what seemed a threatening manner. It was Carlos, the hunchbacked servant of Margaret Lucas, who stood directly in the path of her slow-moving car, forcing her to bring it to a halt. She did so with pounding heart, remembering Ernest's warning against him.

CHAPTER 9

Carlos had left her no choice but to brake the car. Her tension increased as she waited for what would happen next. She had no idea how he came to be out here in the middle of the woods road or why he had chosen to wave her down. But all the memories of his strange actions toward her in the past and the warnings she had been given concerning him came crowding back to fill her with apprehension.

Gripping the wheel fiercely and with her foot poised ready above the gas pedal, she watched him with anxious eyes as he came around to the side window by her.

His grotesquely ugly face wore that usual sneering smile as his powerful hands clenched the frame of the window and he peered in at her.

"You do not look pleased to see me," he taunted her.

"What do you want?" she asked in what she knew was a nervous tone.

He chuckled maliciously. "Miss Victoria does not care to be gracious to a poor cripple."

She had never heard him refer to himself in this manner before. His resentment was as plain as it had ever been, but there was also something else in his manner—something that frightened her.

Trying to appear cool and collected, she looked directly into the leering, ugly face. "I'm in a hurry to get to Collinsport," she said. "I wish you'd explain what you want or let me drive on."

He stared at her. "You have no time for Carlos?"

"I have no patience for the way you're behaving!"

He chuckled again. "That is good!"

"Please!" she begged him now. "I want to get on my way."

"So you may go," he said. "But you must deliver a message for Carlos. Tell the service station operator at the head of the Main Street that I have a flat tire and no spare. I need him to bring his truck to my assistance with a new tire. He knows me; I take the car there."

Victoria felt relief flow through her. She could not hide her new feeling of ease. Nodding, she said, "I'll be glad to do that the moment I reach town."

But Carlos did not remove those powerful hands from the window ledge. He continued to grin at her insolently. "You do not look so worried now."

"What do you mean?"

"You worry that maybe Carlos was another Phantom Mariner?" he inquired in his mocking way.

Some of the relief drained away. "I was surprised to see you step out from the darkness in front of my headlights."

"You are not happy at Collinwood."

"Why do you say that?" she faltered.

The hunchback went on staring at her. "You are frightened and you are right. You should go away!"

Victoria continued to grip the wheel as she frowned at him. "You sound as if you knew some reason why I should run away?"

"Carlos does not always have to explain." His voice was full of smug enjoyment. "But he sees more than many people think."

"What are you trying to tell me?"

The harsh chuckle came again. "Nothing, except I am stuck here on this lonely road with the car and need help. You will attend to it?"

"I will tell the service man."

At last he released the car and stepped back. "Thank you, Miss Victoria," he said. "You would do well to remember all I have said."

With a final dubious glance at his leering face, she brought her foot down hard on the gas pedal and fairly shot the car forward into the foggy night. As she drove on, she caught a glimpse of his car parked on the left side of the road. He'd evidently been on his way back from Collinsport when he'd had the tire trouble. At least that part of his story had been true.

She soon had to slow her speed again. The heavy mist was as impenetrable as before. It was a strain to bend over the wheel and peer for a scant hint of the winding road. Every so often the fog diminished just a little and she was reassured to find that she was still safe from the treacherous ditches that flanked the road on either side. Already she was worrying about the return journey and condemning her own judgment for deciding to drive into the village on such a night.

At last she reached the junction with the main highway. Although the fog was just as bad as before, at least she had the lights of other cars to give her some guidance and a wide road on which to travel. Traffic was moving slowly; it took her at least twice the usual time to reach the center of the village.

The neon sign of the service station was a blur of red and completely unreadable as she drew close to it. But she knew this was the station Carlos had meant and so paused to give his message to the man on duty. The attendant at once recognized the name.

"I just filled his car with gas an hour ago," he said.

"He's midway along the woods road," Victoria told him out the car window. "He's depending on you to send out a tire by a service truck."

The man nodded. "My boy will be back in a few minutes and I'll get him to take it in the pickup. He thinks it's fun to drive on a night like this!" He shook his head disgustedly as she drove away.

Now she could forget about Carlos and proceed on her own business. But as she headed slowly down the hilly, fog-shrouded street she knew that she couldn't completely put the hunchback out of her mind. Not after his strange warning. If only he would tell her why he thought she should leave Collinwood!

This would be something else for her to discuss with Burke Devlin if she found him. She passed the hotel and did not stop. Something told her that on a dismal night like this she would be more likely to find him at the Blue Whale than anywhere else. The lively, cheerful atmosphere of the bar would make it a haven for drifters on this miserable evening.

As she came to the corner where the Blue Whale was located she discovered that the area was indeed crowded with parked cars—so much so that she had to head the station wagon down a side street and walk back in the wet cold of the fog.

Pushing the glass door of the bar open she entered its noisy, warm confines to find the place jammed. The jukebox was blaring out a pop tune, while a group of the area's younger set were lined up at the bar, laughing and talking loudly to be heard over the general din. She knew from past experience that Burke would not be at the bar itself and so pushed her way past several smiling young fishermen whose tanned faces and twinkling eyes offered her an open invitation to join them. She ignored glances of the youths and the jealous looks of the girls they were with.

At the back of the bar she searched for a sign of Burke. After a moment her efforts were crowned with success as Burke noticed her and got up from a seat in one of the booths and came forward to greet her.

Burke gave her a questioning look. "What brings you to town on a night like this?"

"I didn't think it was so bad when I started out," Victoria said.

"You're lucky you didn't run into a ditch somewhere along the way," he told her. "It's the right kind of night for it."

She looked up at him anxiously. "Are you busy?"

He shook his head and offered her an easy smile. "Just discussing some business matters with an out-of-town employee," he said. "We'd finished, anyway. So he'll be moving on."

"I don't want to interrupt you if it's important," she protested.

"It isn't." He went back to the booth to say something to the man who had been there talking to him. The latter rose at once and with a parting word to Burke, turned to leave.

As he passed her he smiled and tipped his snap-brimmed felt hat. He was a stocky man, with an aggressive beet-red face and thin, rather cruel lips.

Burke waited for her to join him. "Sit down," he said, indicating the seat the man had vacated. As she took her place opposite him, he signaled a waiter and ordered for them. Then he turned his full attention to her.

"Must be something pretty important to bring you in here in this fog," he said, studying her intently.

She blushed under his close appraisal. "Not really. As I said, I didn't realize the fog was so bad when I started. Still, things have been happening."

"What things?"

She told him and wound up her account with her meeting with the hunchback and the strange warning he had given her. She shivered as she said, "I can't say why, but I'm terribly afraid of Carlos."

Burke Devlin looked concerned. "I think you may have a right to be. He could be the one behind all your mysterious accidents and also your ghost. He did refer to the Phantom Mariner tonight."

"But I think that was just one of his macabre jokes," she demurred. "He has an ugly sense of humor."

"It strikes me he's ugly in every respect. You can count yourself lucky you had no trouble with him tonight. It probably didn't suit him to reveal his role in things completely at this time."

"I've been blaming the professor for everything," she said.

"Mark Collins is a strange person," Burke conceded. "He is capable of almost anything. And since it would be in his interests to further the match between his daughter and Ernest, I can see that he has a motive for attacks on you."

"Not to mention the possibility I might be his daughter," Victoria reminded the handsome man.

Burke shook his head. "I've never gone along with that idea."

"I know. But I still think it could be true."

"You'd be wiser to forget it."

Victoria's curiosity was aroused. "You're so definite on the subject I'm almost inclined to think you may know more than you're telling me."

He regarded her seriously. "I have always tried to be completely honest with you," he said. "I want you to believe that."

She was immediately repentant. "I know it," she said. "I feel you are the one sure friend I have here."

"Could it be that this Carlos and Mark Collins have entered into some kind of partnership to threaten you?"

Victoria was startled by the suggestion. "I don't think so. They hadn't even met until the professor arrived at Collins House."

"You're assuming that," Burke Devlin said. "There is always the chance they may have known each other somewhere before. And even if they have just met, there's nothing to say they haven't arrived at some working arrangement. Mark is, as I have observed to you, peculiar and unpredictable."

"Perhaps."

"Carlos seems to know what's going on."

"That is true," Victoria agreed.

"You must be extremely wary of him. And of Mark, as well."

"I mean to be," she said. "And Linda is not making things any easier, with her campaign to win Ernest."

"I don't think you'll have any trouble there. Especially since Ernest has made it plain he is merely tolerating her."

"He might change his mind."

"I doubt it," Burke Devlin said. "I think Elizabeth's idea of a costume party is a good one. It should provide some pleasure for you all and maybe ease the tension at Collinwood."

"I think that is what she has in mind," Victoria agreed.

"Have you discussed your problem with Elizabeth?"

"She knows most of the things that have happened. I'm sure she blames the professor. She made that clear the other day when she came to my rescue on the roof."

Burke sighed. "Elizabeth is a good woman, but a strange one. She is apt to be too considerate when it comes to her brothers. She has put up with far too much where Roger is concerned and I think she'd even try to protect Mark if she knew he was involved in something that wasn't right. Keep that in mind."

"I will," she promised.

"I'll drive ahead of you on the way home," he suggested. "You'll have my tail lights to guide you and I can be sure that you come to no harm along the way."

"I don't want to put you to that trouble," she protested.

"I'll worry if I don't do it," he said. "It's only a short distance and I'm a veteran of driving on foggy nights."

In spite of her protests, she was grateful for his help and felt much less nervous on the dark, mist-shrouded road with Burke in his car ahead of her. He drove all the way up to the house and waited until she parked her car. Then he got out of his own car and saw her to the door.

"You'll be all right now," he said.

"Thanks to you," she said, smiling at him in the darkness of the front steps.

He waited until she went inside before returning to his car. She stood by the window next to the door and watched him drive off slowly toward the village. She knew it would be a difficult and tedious journey for him and again felt gratitude for the kindness he had shown her.

But then, Burke Devlin had always been especially good to her. With a warm glow of satisfaction she began to slowly mount the stairway with its single small night light. Burke did not seem to feel she need fear Linda as a rival but did he really know enough about the situation?

Still, he was probably right. Ernest's first great love was his music and he wasn't a playboy type. He said he loved her; and she was ready to accept him at his word. Linda's unfortunate crush on him would vanish when she definitely discovered that Ernest was not interested in her. Thus preoccupied, Victoria neared the first landing.

She was in no way prepared for the appalling sequence of events about to overtake her.

She had barely set foot on the landing when she saw the figure emerge from the shadows—the familiar, dark-cloaked figure that at once sent icy fear racing through her. It was the Phantom Mariner again!

Now he advanced toward her, blocking her avenue to the second flight of stairs and opening his cowl to reveal his grinning skull head. Victoria was paralyzed with fright. She stood there staring at the gruesome apparition, her mouth agape and her eyes wide with terror. She had been so certain that once she was safely in the house she would be all right that she had forgotten about the possible hazards of its shadowed corridors.

The cowled skull came closer and a skeleton hand raised what seemed to be a walking stick. Victoria took it all in with the dazed reaction of the completely hypnotized. Then the walking stick lashed forward. She screamed in pain and terror and toppled backward down the stairway.

Victoria was certain she heard a peal of maniacal laughter as she fell. She blacked out when her head struck a stair.

When she opened her eyes, she was looking up into the face of Roger bending worriedly over her. He was patting her hand and saying something she couldn't understand at first.

"Can you hear me? Victoria, are you all right?"

She studied him with dazed eyes. "The phantom," she said in a small voice.

Roger frowned and let her hand go. "What are you trying to tell me?"

Her senses returned with a rush and she sat up suddenly. "The Phantom Mariner," she said in near hysteria. "He attacked me on the first landing and struck me with his walking stick."

Roger, in his dressing gown, stared down at her with obvious disgust. "Don't go on such drivel! There is no such thing! All that rot about the Phantom Mariner is pure fantasy on the professor's part. He likes to tell spooky stories and he victimized you with this one."

"No!" she protested and turned to stare up at the landing, terror showing on her pretty face. "I did meet the ghost up there."

"I knew no good would come of all that loose talk about phantoms," Roger said angrily as he helped her to her feet. "You may as well admit the truth. Your imagination got the better of you, and in your fright you tripped on the stairs and fell down here." He paused, adding solicitously, "You're sure you're not hurt?"

"No more than a few bruises at most," she assured him, rubbing her head. Raising her eyes to the landing once more, she added, "But what I told you about seeing the ghost was real. And so was the blow he gave me with his walking stick."

Roger regarded her incredulously. "I'm sorry. I just can't accept your story."

"It's true," Victoria said unhappily. She started up the stairs again to the point where she'd encountered the weird phantom figure.

Roger followed a step behind her, complaining, "If you'd just be reasonable, you'd know that such things as the Phantom Mariner simply don't exist. The professor has made his living lecturing and writing about ghosts and mentalism. But you mustn't take his word that such things are true. They are simply part of his bag of tricks."

"You think so?" Victoria said, unable to hide the note of triumph in her voice. "Then what about this?" And she pointed to a black walking stick that still rested on the carpet of the landing.

Roger blinked with annoyance as he studied the stick. "You claim the phantom used this to strike you?"

"Yes."

"First time I've ever known a ghost to arm itself with a walking stick," he said.

Victoria bent to pick it up and examine it. "It's the identical one. He left it behind him."

She held it up for Roger to view it more closely. "Do you recognize it?"

"I think I do," Roger said. "I believe it is the same one the professor had when he came here."

"I'm sure it is!" Victoria agreed.

Roger scowled and took the walking stick from her. "It begins to look as if we've finally hit on the identity of your phantom. I intend to question Professor Mark Veno about this at once."

"But he'll only deny knowing anything about it," she protested.

"At least, let us hear what he has to say for himself," Roger said grimly and led the way up the gloomy second flight of stairs.

Victoria went along with him unwillingly, feeling that nothing would be accomplished by the confrontation. She wished it had been Elizabeth who'd found her, rather than the obstinate Roger. Her body ached painfully from the fall and her mind still had a terrifyingly vivid impression of the Phantom Mariner as he had advanced toward her. Had it been the professor wearing a disguise? It seemed highly probable, although she had no doubt he would deny it. But then, why would he have left his cane behind to identify himself as her attacker? It was too easy! There had to be more to it!

Roger muttered angrily about such things happening at this unholy late hour and led her to the door of the professor's room. "We'll soon know what he's been up to," Roger predicted as he knocked loudly.

A sleepy voice called, "Coming!" And after a moment, the door opened and Professor Veno stood there looking sleepy and disheveled, his dressing-gown thrown on hastily and his skimpy locks of black hair in wild disarray.

He regarded them with some confusion. "What is it?"

Roger held the black walking stick up. "This yours?"

The professor frowned at it. "It could be," he admitted. "At least I have one very much like it."

"Would you kindly let me see it," Roger said grimly.

Looking even more surprised, the professor questioned him with his eyes. Raising a hand to brush his hair in its usual place across his bald pate, he said, "If you'll give me a minute I'll get it." And he vanished into his room again.

Roger gave her a knowing glance. "We'll soon find out what's been going on."

Victoria was not at all as hopeful as Roger was. The professor wouldn't have left the cane behind as evidence against him unless he had a reason for doing so and she couldn't think what it might be. But she was too miserable to utter even a mild protest.

Then the professor was back in the doorway with a troubled expression on his bony, sallow face. "I can't find my walking stick," he admitted. "It seems that must be mine. May I examine it?"

"By all means," Roger said sarcastically. "I thought you'd recognize it sooner or later."

The professor didn't appear to be listening to him. He took the stick and weighed it carefully in his hand and then examined its head. He looked at them both with his burning eyes showing no signs of sleep any longer.

"It is my cane," he announced. "Where did you find it and why are you both here with it at this hour of the night?"

Roger smiled nastily. "Glad to answer your questions. I just hope you'll have ready answers for ours. The cane was found on the first landing where Victoria claims the Phantom Mariner attacked her with it."

Professor Veno showed no surprise. The too-bright eyes met hers. He said, "Is this true, Miss Winters?"

She nodded slowly. "Yes. It came out of the shadows. I saw the skull face. Then the cane was raised. I felt a great surge of pain and I fell backward."

The professor was silent a moment. Then he said, "It would seem someone was playing a prank on you."

"Damn silly kind of prank!" Roger snapped. "She could have broken her back or her neck on those stairs if she hadn't been lucky."

"I still say she was the victim of a practical joke," the professor maintained. "And I can explain why you felt sudden pain from contact with the walking stick. It was not as result of a ghostly touch, nor were you struck by it."

"What are you talking about?" Roger demanded belligerently. It was evident he was annoyed as much at missing his sleep as about the attack on her.

"I'll be glad to explain if you'll give me a moment," the professor said without showing any sign of being upset. He held up the walking stick. "To begin with, this is no ordinary walking stick."

"Obviously not, since it is carried about by a phantom!" Roger said with sarcasm. "You'll have to do better than that!"

"I will," the Professor said. "This stick is actually a weapon that I have carried on my travels for defensive purposes. It is loaded with batteries and when a concealed switch is pressed it gives off a strong electric shock."

"An electric shock!" Roger repeated in a startled tone.

"That is correct," his brother said in his same acid manner. "Someone in the house must have discovered the secret of the stick and decided to use it against Miss Winters. I'm profoundly sorry that it got out of my hands and served such a purpose."

Roger frowned. "You're asking us to believe that someone took the stick from your room?"

"How else could it have gotten down there?" the professor asked. And to Victoria, he said, "Wouldn't you describe the pain you felt as the result of an electric shock?"

"It might have been," she admitted. "I was too startled and terrified to think much about it."

"Now you know what took place," the professor told her. "And I would be willing to wager that the phantom you saw tonight was not the real one."

"It looked the same as the figure I've seen before," Victoria said.

"There were no lights on the landing, were there?" the professor said.

"No," she admitted.

"So you couldn't see clearly in any case," the professor pointed out.

"I saw the cowl and the skeleton head."

"You saw what the prankster wished you to see," the professor told her. "I'm afraid you have an enemy in this house, who knew of your previous encounter with the phantom, and devised this trick to torment you."

Roger glared at the thin man. "You're asking us to believe that you've been in your room all the time, that it wasn't you who wielded that cane!"

The professor smiled grimly. "You came directly up here and you both must be aware that you roused me from a sound sleep. And you also must realize that had it been me I'd never have left the cane behind."

"I don't know about that," Roger blustered, but she could tell that his confidence was shaken. He would not push the professor on this point.

Veno's burning eyes met hers again. "I can't tell you how sorry I am. Miss Winters. And I can assure you this weapon will be safely kept under lock for the balance of my stay here, so it cannot be used for any such purpose again."

"Locking the barn door after the horse is stolen, Roger said angrily. "Elizabeth will hear about this and she may want to take some further action in the matter."

"I am always at her disposal," the professor said urbanely. "And now, if you two will kindly excuse me, I'd like to resume my sleep." Bowing, he went inside and closed the door in their faces.

"Damned arrogant, considering his shaky position in this

house!" Roger declared. Then he turned to her. "Nothing we can do about this tonight." he said. "I'll talk to Elizabeth."

Victoria felt a surge of despair. "I don't think that will help," she said. "He'll simply stick to the same story he told just now."

"I'm not convinced he's telling the truth," Roger assured her. "I'll see you safely to your own room anyhow."

With the door bolted, Victoria slowly began preparing for bed. She still ached from her fall and she was suffering from shock. She had not fully accepted the professor's version of what had happened. But even so, she was beginning to feel the shadow of suspicion had suddenly shifted to Carlos. Remembering his malevolent grin and taunting words, she was willing to believe she might have been the victim of an evil joke on his part.

CHAPTER 10

Bright sunshine flooded her room when Victoria awoke and went down to breakfast. She found Elizabeth already in the kitchen. From the look the older woman gave her as she entered, Victoria decided that she must have already heard about the events of the previous night from Roger.

This was confirmed when Elizabeth said, "I know about your accident."

"I thought you would," she said, waiting.

Elizabeth's attractive matronly face showed concern. "What a stupid thing for anyone to do. You might have been killed."

"I don't know what would have happened if Roger hadn't turned up just then," Victoria said.

The older woman nodded. "And it was the professor's walking stick that was used against you."

"Yes."

"Still, I can't believe he had anything to do with it, even though Roger is suspicious of him," Elizabeth said, siding with her brother, as Victoria had rather expected.

"It was a nightmare, whoever or whatever was responsible," Victoria said simply. "I'm beginning to believe I should leave here."

Elizabeth frowned. "You mustn't feel that way. I want you to stay. We all do."

"Even so, at the rate things have been happening, I don't feel safe in the house anymore. Someone here clearly means me harm."

"Let me take care of that," Elizabeth told her. "And don't you worry. It will be all right. We must begin preparations for the costume party today. I want it to be an outstanding success."

At the moment Victoria found herself with little interest in the proposed party. She felt it would be a great deal more to the point if Elizabeth launched an investigation into the attacks on her at once. Perhaps Elizabeth was apprehensive of what a thorough search into matters might produce. Yet, Victoria thought, she at least should discuss the questioning of the chauffeur, Carlos.

Victoria took her breakfast alone. When the dishes were done she sat with Elizabeth in the library while the older woman began shaping up the list of those who would be invited to the party.

"I don't want too many people," she told Victoria. "But there are some people who must be invited."

Victoria sat politely by and assisted her employer when she could. At the end of an hour and a half session it seemed that at least forty invitations must go out.

Elizabeth sat back with a sigh. "I would prefer half that many, but I've cut the list to the bone."

Victoria pointed out, "Not all of them will be able to come."

"That's a comforting thought," her employer agreed. "We may not actually have more than thirty, which would be a pleasing number added to those of us already in the house." She offered her a smile. "Do you realize this will be the first adult party held here since the old days? Of course I've had children's parties for the youngsters but this will be the first true affair since my husband left." It was seldom she mentioned her missing husband, and Victoria felt a certain embarrassment in attempting a reply.

She settled for, "I'm sure it will be good for all of us."

"I've decided the costumes should be of the period when the house was first built," Elizabeth went on. "So you'll have to make yourself up something along the order of those dresses shown in the older portraits. I'm sure you'll look wonderful in nineteenth-century clothes."

"Do you plan on music?" Victoria asked.

Elizabeth smiled. "Of course. We must have dancing. There is a group in Ellsworth I'm sure we can hire for the occasion. I'll phone Carolyn and ask her to speak to them about it." The older woman paused. "Well, I think that's all we can do this morning. Why don't you take a walk in the air before lunch?"

Victoria was glad to avail herself of the opportunity. It was after eleven and she knew that Linda would be over at the cottage reading to Margaret Lucas, so if Ernest happened to be around they could talk without any fear of being interrupted. She hurried from the library and went out the side door.

Ernest was sitting in one of the chairs on the patio, wearing sunglasses and reading the local newspaper. As soon as he saw her he put the paper down and rose to greet her.

"I've been wanting to see you," he said, his handsome face worried. "Roger told me about last night."

She smiled ruefully. "It seems he told everyone."

"He was very put out about it and so am I," Ernest assured her. "Do you really think it was that fellow Carlos? That seemed to be Roger's opinion."

Victoria shrugged. "I can't say. It all happened so fast. And it was dark. It was the same phantom figure I saw before. And the walking stick that was left there belonged to Professor Veno."

Ernest studied her closely. "You think it could have been the professor?"

"I was sure of it," she admitted. "But then the stick being left there made it seem unlikely."

"That could be why he deliberately left it behind," Ernest pointed out. "You know how crafty he is."

"It's a real possibility."

Ernest frowned. "Still, we shouldn't dismiss Carlos. He could fit in it somewhere. I understand he had tire trouble last night and got in very late."

"I know," she said. "I delivered a message for help to the service station."

"It seems to me you might be better away from here."

"I'm beginning to believe the same thing," she admitted. "I spoke to Elizabeth about it, but she doesn't want me to leave."

"Naturally not. She's lonely here with Carolyn at school. But she should think of you."

"Things were normal enough until the Professor arrived," Victoria said. "I was a little afraid of Carlos but he hadn't bothered me. It is only since Linda and her father came here that I've been having these mysterious incidents."

"Then that would seem to indicate all the trouble you've encountered is linked with the professor."

"That's how I feel. He was the only person to mention the legend of the Phantom Mariner and it was after he told me the story that I first saw the ghost."

Ernest's brow furrowed. "You're sure you didn't allow your imagination to run away with you?"

"No. I really saw it. That first night as the storm was ending I met it on the path between the cottage and here."

"And that was the start of it all?"

"Yes."

"What does Elizabeth say about it?"

"I think she wants to protect the professor," Victoria said. "She is very fond of her brothers."

"I hope not so fond that she'll allow Mark to attempt murder. That is what these attacks on you amount to."

"I wouldn't want to accuse him on the slight evidence available," Victoria said.

"Still, the bulk of the suspicion must rest on him." Victoria sighed. "I'll stay until you leave, anyway. After that, I don't know. At least I'll be here to help with the party."

Ernest's sensitive face showed worry. "I'm not nearly as enthusiastic about this party as Elizabeth and Linda seem to be. But I suppose that is not too surprising. Still, with what has been going on here I'd think Elizabeth should first concern herself with finding out what is behind it all."

"She has promised that she is going to do just that."

"Do you believe her?"

"I want to," Victoria said. "I'm not sure."

"Exactly the way I feel," Ernest agreed. "Shall we take a stroll?"

This time they took the path down to the wharf where they were safely out of sight of the house. They stood on the ancient gray timber jetty where Roger's motor cruiser was tied and stared out at the calm silver ocean of this bright noon. Then Ernest gently took her in his arms for a long kiss.

As he let her go he said solemnly, "I'm afraid for you. I don't trust Mark Collins."

She looked up at him. "Do you think he is trying to kill me or frighten me away so Linda will have a free field with you?"

"He's making a mistake if that's what he has in mind," Ernest said grimly. "Linda is nothing more than a friend, as far as I'm concerned."

"And you've already told her that."

"I have."

"Still, she keeps hoping and trying. It seems to be an obsession with her."

Ernest sighed. "In spite of her traveling and the seeming glamour of her life, she's actually a lonely and frightened girl. I think that is why she so easily misinterpreted my kindness. It's too bad but I've had to be frank with her."

"The professor may have his own ideas on the subject," Victoria pointed out.

Ernest seemed to be in agreement. He said, "I must make it a point to get in a conversation with him and let him plainly understand that I'm not serious about his daughter. When he hears it directly from me he may be convinced that I mean it, regardless of what might happen to you."

"That might be worth trying," she said. As she spoke she let her eyes wander to the path which they had used coming down and the bush-covered hill above them. She caught the sign of a slight movement near one of the bushes and with a sharp intake of breath she gripped Ernest's arm. "Up there!" she said in a tense, low voice.

Startled, he looked up toward the hillside. "I don't see anything."

She was straining her eyes in the direction of the bushes and again she caught a shadow-like figure swiftly moving from one area of thick growth to another for cover. She saw plainly enough to know it was Carlos and that he had been spying on them.

"It's Carlos up there watching us," she said in the same low voice. "I saw him retreating to the bushes near the top just now."

Ernest glared up at the sun-drenched hillside angrily. "I'll go up there and let him have a piece of my mind," he said.

She held him back. "No," she told him. "He probably thinks we weren't able to see who it was. Let him go on thinking that. Maybe we'll find out what he's up to."

He gave her an impatient, dubious glance. "We may not get another chance like this. He must still be up there hiding in that area. Why not have it out with him now?" Victoria wasn't sure of her own reasons for wanting to avoid a showdown, yet she knew that was how she felt. So she said, "Call it an intuition on my part. I think if we interfere with him now we'll lose our opportunity to find out more later."

Ernest continued to study the hillside. "He's probably safely on his way by this time."

"Yes. And he must have a strong reason or he wouldn't be taking the trouble to spy on us."

The young violinist regarded her with fresh concern. "Now it seems that Carlos is tied up with the professor in some way."

"I'm afraid so."

"What a pair they make!" Ernest said grimly. "No wonder you've been having problems!"

She realized she was trembling a little and was aware of what a toll the strain of continuing on in the house of dark shadows was taking from her. She said, "It's almost lunch time. I have to go back and help Elizabeth."

Ernest looked unhappy. "We get so little time together. You're always having to run back to the house to help with one thing or another."

She smiled faintly. "Don't forget I am working here and not a guest or one of the family like you."

He put an arm around her as they began to stroll back and very seriously said, "I think it's close to time you forgot about this job and we began making plans."

She shook her head. "You're only saying that because you're so worried about me."

"Don't analyze my motives," he said. "I mean what I say."

"I'll consider it," she told him lightly. "Just now my biggest problem is getting lunch ready."

The meal proved another trying session. Roger came home from the cannery and helped himself to several martinis before he sat down. As a result, he came to the table in a mean humor. The professor was his usual malevolent self and seemed to be enjoying the tension around the table. Only Linda was completely at ease and in a good mood.

When she got up from the table she paused to tell Victoria, "Mrs. Lucas was asking for you when I was over reading to her this morning. I think she wants to talk to you."

Victoria thanked her. "I'll drop by this afternoon," she promised.

Linda's eyes held a teasing sparkle. "I'm going to see if Roger will allow us to use his boat today. I'd like to have Ernest take me out along the shore as far as Collinsport."

Victoria made no reply as she busied herself gathering up the dishes to take them to the kitchen. She knew that the other girl was deliberately trying to torment her and she wasn't going to rise to the bait. Still, it did bother her a little—especially as she had an idea Roger was continuing his afternoon drinking and would probably quickly agree to their using his cabin cruiser.

When she finished helping Elizabeth with the dishes she went upstairs and changed to a white dress with tiny blue polka dots and a blue scarf collar. She went to the window and searched the cove to see if Roger's boat was out there. It only took her a moment to spot it. Linda had succeeded in her plan after all, she decided bitterly. And no doubt she'd talked Ernest into going with her. The small craft was clearly headed in the direction of Collinsport. Feeling somewhat uneasy about it all, Victoria left the window and went downstairs.

Carlos was standing by the car near the cottage. He touched a forefinger to his gray chauffeur's cap. With the familiar sneering smile on his grotesquely ugly face he said, "Thanks for last night."

She forced herself to pause and ask, "You did get your tire, then?"

"It came," he said. "I had you worried out there, didn't I?"

Pretending a calm she didn't feel, she said, "I don't know what you mean."

"Don't try to fool Carlos. You were scared like crazy," the

hunchback said. "Teach you a lesson not to go driving around alone at night."

Victoria decided to test him. "It seems the house can be equally dangerous."

His eyes mocked her. "I've been telling you that. You won't listen."

"How do you know so much?"

He chuckled unpleasantly. "My people all have second sight. Don't let this hump on my back fool you. I can trace my ancestry direct to a gypsy king."

"Interesting," she said. "In that case you must know a lot about all the ancient black arts. I mean spells and phantoms and secret potions." She was deliberately trying to get him to talk some more.

"I could tell you plenty of things about this place," Carlos promised her, his swarthy face showing a wise expression.

"I wish you would," she encouraged him.

His eyes narrowed craftily. "What good would it do? You never listen to me." And with a final leering smile he got into the car, preparing to drive away.

Realizing that he had been too clever for her, she turned away with a crimson face and continued on to the cottage. When she reached its door she was surprised to find the frail invalid, Margaret Lucas, waiting for her anxiously.

"I saw you had stopped to talk to Carlos," Margaret said by way of explanation. "I was afraid be might be annoying you again."

"No," she assured her. "I just wanted to find out if he got his tire all right last night."

"So that was it!" Margaret Lucas sounded relieved. "He did finally get it, but it was very late when he returned."

"I'm sure it must have been," Victoria said. "It was a dreadfully foggy night."

"I know it, my dear," the invalid said. "And today is so nice. Do let us sit out back in the garden. I sometimes feel starved for air and sunshine."

Victoria allowed herself to be guided around back where two wicker chairs stood on a flagstone area flanking a small flower garden. A black and yellow umbrella table between the chairs offered shelter from the blazing sun.

As soon as they had seated themselves the gray-haired woman leaned across to her and said, "I've missed our conversations and I've been very worried about you. I hear you had fresh trouble last night."

Victoria nodded. Her experience of the previous evening seemed a nightmare as they sat here in this fragrant garden with the lazy buzz of insects in the background. She said, "I saw the Phantom Mariner on the first landing last night."

"Again!"

"Yes," she said. "And this time there was something else to prove that I didn't just imagine it as the others have accused before. A walking stick was left behind. A special kind of walking stick belonging to Professor Mark Veno."

"What sort of walking stick?"

"It's a weapon, actually. It's loaded with slim storage batteries to give off an electric shock when a switch in the handle is pressed. The professor claims to carry it for protection on his travels. The phantom used it on me and I fell down the entire flight of stairs."

Margaret Lucas was aghast. "You could have been killed!"

"Fortunately, I wasn't even badly bruised," she said.

"But how did the cane get there?"

"The professor insists it was stolen from his room. He claims that someone is playing the role of the Phantom Mariner and took the walking stick to use against me."

"In other words, he's saying that someone has been pretending to be this ghost all along with the intention of harming you?"

"Yes."

"Do you believe him?"

"I think it's at least partly true," Victoria admitted. "And either he is doing it himself or he has hired Carlos as an accomplice."

"Carlos! I don't think he'd lend himself to such a thing!" the invalid protested.

"Not even if he was well paid?" Victoria inquired. "The professor has enough money to buy him. I'm sure."

The invalid slumped back in her chair. "All I really know about Carlos is that he is completely loyal to me."

"I don't question that."

"Nor can I imagine him harming a friend of mine. And he knows you are a friend."

"I think it would be different with anyone else," Victoria pointed out. "I don't believe you can count on his loyalty beyond yourself."

"He is a strange person," Margared admitted. "You could be right. If he is the one threatening you I feel extremely guilty."

"There is no reason why you should."

"Because I brought Carlos here in the first place,"

"But it is the professor who may have enlisted him in his campaign against me. So it is the professor who must be blamed if Carlos is involved."

The invalid frowned. "I still say you are wrong. I think it is all professor Veno's doing."

"You may be right. But why would he have left his own walking stick?"

"Maybe he did it deliberately, as a kind of bluff."

"That has been suggested before," Victoria admitted.

"It wouldn't take too clever a mind to work out that scheme," Margaret told her. "And you believe his motive for all this is simply his desire to see his daughter marry Ernest Collins?"

"Either that, or it has something to do with my past."

"The mystery of your own parents."

"Yes."

The invalid appeared to give this some thought. At last she said, "I'm going to make what may appear to be a cold suggestion, but one which might save you from this apparent danger. I'm terribly concerned for your safety."

"What have you in mind?" Victoria asked, sensing that the sick woman was very upset.

The eyes behind the dark glasses fixed on her. There was a long moment of silence and then Margaret said, "Why not give Ernest Collins up?"

Victoria could hardly credit what she heard. "Give up Ernest?"

"Yes," the invalid said quietly. "I warned you what I was about to say might shock you and I see that it has. But I am thinking of you and your safety. Your romance with this young man is not as important as your life."

"But we love each other!"

"That won't mean much if you are killed because of the romance."

"There must be some other way."

"I doubt it, as long as Linda continues to show an interest in the young man. Her father will risk anything to see that she wins him. I think I understand the sort of person Professor Veno is."

"I could leave Collinwood and I think I will," Victoria said.

"That would merely postpone your rendezvous with the Phantom Mariner, unless I miss my guess. The professor would find you and eliminate you, wherever you might go."

"But Ernest is not in love with Linda," she protested. "It's too preposterous."

"She could make him fall in love with her if you weren't on the scene as a rival," Margaret suggested. "She is an attractive girl and decidedly in love with him. I sit here day after day while she goes on about him."

Victoria, realizing Margaret Lucas had only her welfare at heart, tried to restrain the slight anger she felt. "I'm sorry," she said. "I don't think I could do what you suggest. I'm too much in love with Ernest myself."

The invalid studied her sadly. "It is a predicament, isn't it?"

"I'm afraid so."

"Forgive what must seem very much like impudence on my part," Margaret said. "It is hard to sit by helplessly and see those of whom you are fond hurt. I only meant to be helpful."

Victoria was touched. "Of course I understand that," she said quickly.

"So it seems the drama must play on to its finish. I do beg you to be careful, my dear."

Victoria was curious for information about Linda. She said, "You feel sure Linda is as much in love with Ernest as before?"

"I'm certain of it. She can't seem to talk about anything but him. Oh, she has mentioned the costume party Mrs. Stoddard is planning, but only now and then."

"I see," Victoria said, more worried than ever. "She still hopes to change Ernest's mind. There's no question of that. She talked him into taking her out in the boat this afternoon."

"I've warned you," Margaret Lucas said. "She is a lovely girl. Ernest Collins would have to be blind not to be aware of her charm."

"He does like her and admire her. But he doesn't love her. At the most all he ever felt for her was pity."

The invalid smiled wearily. "Have you any idea how close pity is to love, my dear?"

Victoria was increasingly alarmed by the suggestion that Linda might have a better chance with Ernest than she had ever suspected. Could Linda have divulged some secrets to the sick woman which she didn't know?

And suddenly Victoria found herself wondering about Ernest. She had never expected to doubt him, but she was beginning to think there was more going on than she was aware of. Could Ernest be playing a double game?

Placating each of them with the same story? Was that why Margaret Lucas had suggested she break up with him? Was the sick woman trying to let her down without too much hurt?

Suddenly she felt ill at ease and anxious to get away so she might sort out her troubled thoughts. Rising quickly, she said, "It's getting late. I must go."

The sick woman looked forlorn. "But surely you'll stay to have tea with me?"

"Thank you, no," Victoria said with an attempt at a smile. "I seem to have a headache. It may be the sun. I'd like to take a little rest before dinner."

Margaret rose to her feet with effort. "I do hope I haven't upset you with my foolish talk," she worried.

"Not at all," Victoria said. "I know that you thought it for the best."

"Please believe that," Margaret said solemnly and she came

closer to touch her arm. "I'm only sorry I haven't been able to help you more. And please, do be careful of that dreadful professor."

"I will," Victoria said, and hurried back in the direction of Collinwood.

Her mind was a confusion of tormented thoughts. When she reached the rear entrance of the towering, dark house she decided not to go in. She couldn't face her misery in its shadowy coldness. So she proceeded on across the lawn to the path that ran parallel with the cliff. Without actually thinking, she went beyond this to the start of the path leading down to the wharf.

It was then she came back to reality with a start and halted. The cabin cruiser was there tied in its usual place and standing on the deck were Linda and Ernest Collins. This fact didn't surprise her too much, but what did upset her was the sight of them locked in a tight embrace.

She stood there for a moment, hope draining away from her. Margaret Lucas had been right. Linda was a more dangerous rival than she had ever guessed. Sick at what she had seen, she turned quickly to start up the path again.

And now she gasped aloud. Standing directly in her path was the weird, black-garbed figure of Professor Mark Veno. The bony, sallow face wore a sarcastic smile and the wide-brimmed black hat was pulled down well on his forehead.

Eyes burning into hers, he said, "You'd better accept the situation, Miss Winters, however bitter it may be for you."

CHAPTER 11

Tears were brimming in Victoria's eyes. Without replying, she dodged past him and stumbled up the path, then hurried across the lawn to Collinwood and went directly upstairs to her own room.

After a good cry she repaired her face and went down to help Elizabeth with dinner. If the older woman noticed that she was not quite herself, she made no acknowledgement of the fact. The ordeal became almost unbearable when Victoria had to join the others at the dinner table. One glance at the sardonic, smiling face of the professor was enough—and both Ernest and Linda seemed in unusually high spirits. She avoided looking at them as much as possible.

Roger was irritable after a day of more than average drinking and scowled at Ernest across the dinner table. "You tie my boat up properly after you brought it back?"

"I was very careful," Ernest said.

"He really was. Uncle Roger," Linda said with a fetching smile for the older man. "And I checked the boat myself to be certain."

"Trouble with amateurs is that they never know when they've done a thing properly or not," Roger grumbled over his heaping plate of roast beef, seeming not at all impressed by their assurances.

Elizabeth inquired, "Did you two have a nice afternoon on the water?"

"It was wonderful!" Linda told her in a tone of smug happiness that made Victoria wince.

"The view is great from the water," Ernest said. "It's a very interesting shoreline."

Victoria felt like telling them the view had also been revealing from where she had stood on the hillside. But she said nothing, not wanting to risk tears again.

At last dinner ended and she helped Elizabeth carry out the dishes. But the mistress of Collinwood refused to let her help wash them. "You've done enough for today," she said. "Go out and join the others and enjoy yourself."

It was the last thing Victoria wanted to do, but Elizabeth would not listen to her protests. So she found herself slowly advancing along the corridor toward the front of the old house. As she came to the library she paused. Seeing the big room was empty, she went in there for a refuge. She could hear the voices of the others from the living room as she faced one of the walls lined with bookshelves from floor to ceiling.

She began studying the ancient volumes that made up much of the library and from time to time drew one from the shelf to riffle through its pages. The pungent odor of age and dampness assailed her nostrils as she examined the old books and she forgot some of her depression as her interest in them grew.

One of the volumes was a history of the county in which Collinwood stood. Skimming through the contents, she became aware that the Collins name figured prominently in the account of the area. She was completely absorbed in a description of the dipper ship trade when she suddenly heard the library door dose. With a startled expression she glanced in toward the door to discover that Ernest had entered and closed it behind him for privacy.

Now he came over to her with a puzzled smile on his sensitive face and asked, "What sort of game have you been trying to play on me this evening?"

She closed the book and put it back on the shelf, avoiding looking directly at the young man. She shrugged, "I don't know what you mean."

He took her firmly by the arms and turned her facing him. "Yes, you do. I hope you're not sulking because I took Linda out in that boat. I couldn't very well not do it. I've been avoiding her for days."

Victoria held her chin high. "I'm sure you didn't want to refuse her."

"It was just a harmless boat ride," he argued. "It didn't mean anything. Surely you're not going to be angry about it."

"And it had such a happy ending!" she taunted him.

His expression changed to a look of guilt. Victoria felt ill all over again. However much he might deny it, she had caught him making love to Linda. She waited to hear whether he would lie to her.

"You saw us then?" he said with surprising candor. He didn't sound happy but he didn't sound apologetic either.

"I saw you on the deck," she said.

"That was Linda's fault."

"You're not being very gallant," she reprimanded him coldly.

"I don't mean to be," he said with a hint of anger. "Linda was responsible for what you saw. She literally threw herself in my arms."

"It seemed a cooperative venture from where I watched," Victoria said.

Now Ernest looked miserable. "I tell you, I was just as surprised as you must have been. One moment she was standing there smiling at me and the next she was pressed close to me with her arms around my neck."

"How upsetting!" she said with heavy sarcasm.

"It was for me," he insisted. "I was so surprised I guess I did return her kiss and then I got untangled from her as fast as I could. She laughed and teased me about it and that's all there was to it."

"You expect me to believe that?"

His grip on her arms tightened so that she felt pain. "I've told you the truth. You've got to believe it!"

"Linda seemed unusually happy at dinner."

"Because she thought she had put something over on me," he said. "I'll not let myself be caught in a spot like that again. I promise you." And saying this, he brought her close for a kiss.

She wanted to believe he was telling the truth. The chances were that he had. But damage had been done to their relationship. She knew it might be some time before she would be willing to trust him completely again; she couldn't relax in his arms.

He looked down at her with a troubled expression. "I'm sorry you had to see what happened and that it upset you."

"You'd rather I hadn't known anything about it, I suppose."

"Frankly, yes."

Victoria studied him solemnly. "I wonder how many other incidents like this I've missed? A great many of them in Spain, I'd be willing to bet."

He let her arms go and stared at her. "Then you'd bet wrong," he said. "You're making entirely too much of what happened."

She saw that she had been wrong in pursuing the subject now that he had offered her his version of it. She forced a small smile and said, "Very well. Consider yourself forgiven."

"Thanks," he said bitterly. "I know that's just on the surface. You really haven't made up your mind yet. But I'll prove I was telling the truth, if you'll give me time enough."

"We won't say anything more about it," she said. And with a sudden inspiration she added, "Anyway, I haven't time to talk about it anymore. I'm going into town tonight."

He frowned. "To see your millionaire friend, Burke Devlin, I suppose. That fellow is much too rich and handsome for me to enjoy having you meet him so often."

It was her turn to scoff. "Don't be ridiculous!" she said lightly as she started for the door.

He followed her. "I'll drive you in. Don't forget all the trouble you had the other night."

"I'll not have any tonight," she said firmly. "There's no fog and I'd much rather go alone in the station wagon."

She didn't wait to hear his objections but hurried out of the library to ask Elizabeth for permission to use the station wagon. As she expected, the older woman agreed and within a matter of minutes she was behind its wheel and heading for the village.

Because she hadn't thought about making the trip until the last moment she had no idea whether Burke Devlin would be in Collinsport or not. But she decided to try the hotel first. They would probably be able to tell her where he'd gone if he wasn't there.

As it turned out, he was the first person she saw in the lobby of the shabby little hostelry. Burke was talking to the desk clerk as she entered. He smiled when he saw her, and came over.

"I can almost tell when you'll arrive and the exact time," he said. "I had a hunch you'd be in tonight."

"I only decided to come at the last moment," she said.

"I'm on my way out of town," he told her. "But I'll stay a half-hour and we can have a coffee together before I leave."

They went into the hotel coffee shop and took a corner table suitably remote from the several other couples already in there. Burke stared at her over his steaming cup of coffee.

"What's the big problem tonight?" he wanted to know.

"All the old ones have grown a little larger," she said.

"Sounds bad."

"It is."

"You'll survive," he promised her. "You have before."

"I saw Ernest and Linda in each other's arms," she said. Burke raised his eyebrows.

"That must have come as a shock!"

"It did. Ernest claims it was all an accident."

He smiled. "Sometimes accidents like that do happen." So she quickly brought him up to date on all the happenings at Collinwood. As he listened, his handsome face reflected his growing concern. He made no comment, until she had completed her account of events.

Frowning, he commented, "I thought I'd seen you safely home the other night. I hadn't counted on you being attacked in the house."

"You couldn't be expected to guess that."

"I don't like this business of the walking stick," Burke went on. "I'd say that Mark Collins left it there purposely to throw off the scent. It's my guess he's your Phantom Mariner."

"You could easily be right."

"And what do you think of your friend, Ernest?"

Victoria sighed. "I don't know. I want to believe him."

"But do you?"

"Not completely. It will be a long while until I'm sure."

Burke raised an eyebrow. "Perhaps your invalid woman friend was right when she advised you to consider giving Ernest up. Are you sure he's worth the effort and danger?"

She smiled forlornly. "I'm afraid I still think so."

"You're not easily advised," Burke said. "I'm going to worry about you when I'm away."

"Will you be gone long?"

"I'll be back in time for the party," he promised. "A few days before it, probably."

"Burke," she said awkwardly, "can you find out some more about Mark Collins?"

"Such as?"

"What he did when he first left here. Before he became Professor Mark Veno. I'd like to know more about that first wife of his and if both she and the baby did actually die at childbirth."

Burke sighed. "So you're off on that again. Still trying to tag yourself with a Collins parentage. I'd hoped you were cured."

"There is a mystery about my origins," she said. "You can't blame me for wanting to discover the truth."

"I can blame you for having pipe dreams and thinking a rotter like Mark Collins might be your father. If that was the case, why would he be trying to kill you?"

She shrugged. "Because he thinks more of Linda and her happiness than he does mine."

"It doesn't fit," Burke Devlin said. "But I'll be in New York tomorrow. I'll speak to the private detective agency that has done some work for me and ask them to dig around for some facts about the professor. Will that satisfy you?"

She brightened. "Thanks, Burke!" Blushing, she added, "You may be interested to learn that Ernest is jealous of you."

Burke laughed. "That builds my ego considerably. I only wish he had more reason to be."

Then glancing at his watch, he said, "I'm afraid I'll have to leave now. I have a long drive ahead of me."

He saw her to her car and then she headed back to Collinwood. It was clear, with a moon and plenty of stars and the road held no surprises for her that night. When she finally reached the old house, all was quiet there. She parked the station wagon and went into the dimly lighted house and up to her room without seeing anyone. Not even the Phantom Mariner.

The next days were busy ones as she helped Elizabeth send out invitations and make preparations for the party. They planned to do much of the fancy cooking ahead, freeze the various delicacies and take them from the freezer the night of the party. She had never seen Elizabeth so enthusiastic about anything before.

"You won't have to worry about making up a costume after all," she told Victoria. "There are at least a dozen big trunks filled with old clothing up in the attic. I'll give you the keys to the storage rooms and when Carolyn comes home on Saturday you, she, and Linda can go up there and take your pick. There is bound to be something right for you."

Elizabeth's pretty, teen-age daughter was even more excited than the rest of them about the costume party. When she came home on the weekend she took an active role in the planning of the event and early Saturday evening they all went up to the attic to search through the trunks.

Carolyn led the way, armed with her mother's keys. She confided to Victoria and Linda, "This is the first time Mother has even let me have these keys. There must be really fabulous things up here."

Linda sighed. "I don't care whether I find a fabulous dress or not, just so long as it fits and is the right color."

"There is bound to be a selection," Victoria said, feeling she should make some comment. She had talked little with Linda since the boat episode earlier in the week. Ernest had also been much subdued in recent days. He had kept to his own room a lot, explaining that he was working hard at his concerto. Victoria had the idea he was using this as an excuse to keep out of Linda's way. He wanted to break the bridge of intimacy that had grown between them.

Carolyn went ahead down the narrower attic corridor and found the right key for the first of the storage rooms. It proved to be fairly small with a low ceiling and a single, cobwebbed window. There was no electricity on this floor so they would need to use the early evening light that came in through the murky window. There were at least a half-dozen large trunks with rounded tops, and cardboard boxes securely tied with cord were stored on top of some of them.

Carolyn approached the nearest of the trunks and knelt to open it. "We may as well begin here," she said, as the odor of mothballs filled the room.

She had selected a good one. The clothes were suitably old, but nearly unworn. Carolyn found a pink evening gown with gorgeous frills almost at once and shortly afterward Linda produced a lively blue gown with gold trimming that seemed a perfect fit. Both girls were so delighted with their finds that they immediately took the dresses down to Elizabeth for discussions about alterations.

This left Victoria alone in the dreary little room to continue searching for something her own size and type. One by one she took out the carefully folded items, shook them out and rejected them. But the trunk was well-filled, so she kept at her task and was rewarded when she discovered a lovely rose gown at the very bottom of it. Delicate beige lace formed frills on the tight sleeves and low neck. She held it up for size; it would require only the most minor alterations along with an airing and a good press. She had her dress at last.

So occupied had she been with her search she hadn't noticed the time passing. The dim light of the room and the sight of dusk through the windows told her she had completed her task none too early. She had expected Carolyn to return and see to locking up the room, but apparently the girls had become so caught up in their plans for altering their dresses they'd forgotten all about it. Well, no harm would be done in leaving the room open until the morning.

Quickly she put the other things back in the trunk and closed its fid. She picked up the rose silk dress and was on the point of turning to leave when the door of the room was suddenly closed on her.

"Carolyn, I'm still in here!" she called out, going to the door. But even as she spoke the key was being turned and there was no reply.

Still holding the dress, she stared at the panels of the wooden door with growing alarm. The room was almost in darkness and she had been accidentally locked in there. Or had she?

"Carolyn!" she called again in an agitated voice and this time she rattled the knob hard in a futile effort to open it. Only a mocking silence answered her worried cry.

Panic welled up in her as she stood there in the musty room with its relics of other days. Every minute the shadows grew thicker. She couldn't understand what had happened and why Carolyn had locked the door without noticing her still in there. Surely they must have missed her!

She glanced about her as the growing darkness made the outlines of the boxes and trunks take on the menacing appearance of ghostly figures. She was trembling and unable to think clearly.

Again she turned to pound the door with a clenched fist. "Carolyn!" she shouted. "Carolyn! Please let me out!" But there was only the quiet that had answered her other pleas for help.

She slumped against the door, staring at the ominous shadows of the long abandoned room. Darkness was showing outside the window and she was finding it hard to see anything clearly. She still clutched the gown she'd discovered, although her mind had long since dismissed it in her terrifying need to escape.

Her own nervous breathing became a sound filling her ears as she waited there in the blackness of the small room. She was sick with fear and began to grope her way across the crowded floor to reach the single tiny window. Even if she couldn't escape through it she might open it or break the glass and shout for help until someone below heard her.

She stumbled and painfully hit a shin as she slowly edged around the trunks and boxes of the well-filled room. It seemed to take an eternity to reach the window and as she did so she fumbled with the window sash, to see if it would raise. It resisted. She began to think she would have to smash the glass in the lower casing.

As she hesitated over this, there was a slight but definite rustling sound from behind her in the dark. An icy dagger of fear plunged through her. She was not alone in the room! The rustling sound came clearly again and she pressed close to the wall, so frozen by terror that she was unable to move or cry out. She was locked in this musty room with an unknown horror!

The faint rustling drew closer. She heard a box move on the floor near her. Her wide, staring eyes searched the blackness of the tiny room for a sign of the thing that was bearing down on her, but she could see nothing. Her heart was pounding with terror and her breath was coming in odd, uneven gasps.

And then she heard the sound from outside. The key turned in the lock and the door was thrown open. "Victoria! Where are you?" It was Carolyn's clear young voice.

With a strangled sob of relief Victoria rushed across the room to join the other girl.

"What happened?" Carolyn wanted to know. "We realized you hadn't come down so I came up here to get you. I found the door closed and the key turned in the lock."

Victoria explained weakly, "Someone shut the door and locked me in."

"But who?"

She shook her head. "I don't know." And with a tiny shudder she stared back into the pitch-dark room. "There was something in there with me."

"What?" Carolyn's tone was sharply incredulous.

Victoria looked at her solemnly. "It's true. I heard a strange rustling. It came closer all the time. I couldn't see anything. I think I'd have died of fear if you hadn't come when you did."

Carolyn's pretty young face showed alarm as she gazed into the room. In a hushed tone, she said, "Let's get away from here!" And she slammed the door quickly, turned the key again and then removed it.

They were heading for the stairs in the grim shadows when they heard a moan from down the corridor ahead of them. They halted and Carolyn clutched her arm. "Did you hear that?"

"Yes!" Victoria's voice was a whisper.

And as she spoke the moan was repeated more loudly. There was no question now that it came from the narrow hallway leading to the stairs. And Victoria knew there was no other avenue of escape at this level of the old house. The rear stairway only went as far as the third floor.

"What will we do?" Carolyn quavered, holding onto her arm tightly.

"We'll have to go on. See who it is."

"Suppose it is your ghost?"

Victoria said, "I doubt it. But we have no choice. We're trapped up here."

They advanced silently in the near darkness and then a third moan came, this time from almost at their feet. A moment later Victoria made out the figure outstretched on the floor.

"Someone's been hurt," she said breathlessly, kneeling down. And as the black-clad figure turned with a moan she saw his face. "It's the professor!"

"I'll go get help!" Carolyn said and ran on ahead.

"Professor Veno," Victoria said, touching him on the shoulder. "It's Victoria Winters."

He appeared not to hear her but merely moaned again. She stayed bent over him and finally there came the sound of footsteps and voices approaching up the stairs. A moment later Carolyn was back with Linda, Roger and Elizabeth. Roger was the first to appear with a powerful flashlight which he held over the injured man.

"Got a nasty crack on the head," he said, bending close to him. Then he addressed himself to the professor. "It's Roger! What happened?"

The professor opened his eyes and blinked under the glare of the strong flashlight, a dazed expression on his sallow, bony face. "Where is he?"

"Who?" Roger asked.

"The Phantom Mariner," the professor said. "I saw him just

now."

"Daddy!" Linda cried, pushing her way past the others to kneel beside the stricken man.

Roger straightened up. "He's raving," he said. "Let's get him down from here."

But twenty minutes later, propped up with pillows on a divan in the living room, the professor was just as adamant in his belief that he had seen the legendary ghost. He had refused the services of a doctor and let Elizabeth bandage his head. Now he sat there sipping brandy, the burning eyes alert again as he recounted what had happened.

"I was on the point of entering my own room," he said, "when I saw this shadow move in the hallway. It struck me as odd and because of what had happened to Victoria the other night I decided to investigate."

"And then?" Roger said.

"I found the shadow was a figure cloaked in a dark cape or something of the sort. I followed it up the stairs to the attic. When I was close to it I called out. It turned." He paused. "It was then I saw the grinning skull face that Victoria has described. But only for a moment. The figure fled and vanished in the shadows. I'm sure it dodged into one of the rooms."

"But when were you attacked?"

"Later," the professor said. "I went on down the corridor and on the way back, after I had found no sign of anyone, someone struck me on the head from the rear."

Roger studied him grimly. "Your Phantom Mariner left you a very real reminder of your encounter with him." The professor took another sip of his brandy and nodded slightly. "I'll not soon forget the meeting or that skeleton face."

Ernest, who had been standing between Linda and Victoria, spoke up. "I think it is time we called in the police. Some kind of lunatic is at large on the estate. We can't risk our lives any longer."

The professor's sallow face took on a sardonic grin. "You propose to enlist the services of the police against a phantom?"

"Not a phantom!" Ernest said angrily. "A madman!"

Roger turned on the young violinist coldly. "I believe it is my place to make the decisions here."

Elizabeth, who had been sitting silently in a wing back chair a distance from the divan, now spoke for the first time. "Allow me to disagree, Roger. It has continually been your policy to rest the weight of responsibility here on me."

Her younger brother flushed a deep crimson. "Naturally I planned to consult with you on any move I might make."

"I'm glad to hear that," she said calmly. "I see no need for this wild alarm nor do I plan to expose the family to scandal by asking the police to investigate these happenings."

Victoria was surprised at the quiet but authoritative pronouncement. Once again she recalled Elizabeth's strong tendency to protect her brothers at any cost. Did she suspect more than she was letting on? Could this supposed attack on the professor be another false clue to lead them into thinking he had nothing to do with the mysterious attacks on her? He might even have enlisted the evil Carlos to stage the assault.

Now Professor Veno said, "I agree with Elizabeth. I do not think we should expose our dirty linen to the public. This house has long been known to be frequented by a phantom. Let us accept the situation."

Ernest frowned. "You can say that? Stick with such nonsense after having nearly lost your own life?"

Professor Veno nodded. "Yes."

Elizabeth said, "I think we should all try to put this out of our minds. In due time the situation here will quiet down. Let us concentrate on the party and our plans for it and let this other matter rest."

Roger Collins shrugged. "If that is what you think best."

"It is," Elizabeth said firmly.

Victoria thought the professor looked quietly triumphant as he offered her a mocking smile above his brandy glass. She exchanged frightened glances with Carolyn, unable to imagine that the party would bring any gaiety to the house under these conditions. She was all at once acutely aware of the stench of moth balls and glanced down to see that she was still clutching the silk gown once worn by some long dead female of the Collins line.

CHAPTER 12

The day of the party was as lovely as if they had especially planned the weather. It was typical of the clear, crisp late September familiar to Maine. In the final days of preparation and planning everyone in the house except Professor Veno had been drawn into the work and excitement. Linda had taken charge of the decorating while Victoria concentrated on helping Elizabeth with preparing the food.

Carolyn returned from school in Ellsworth on Friday evening and so was able to assist Linda with the last-minute decorations. And Elizabeth, whose milk-white skin bore mute evidence to the fact she had not been exposed to outside sun or weather, during the nearly twenty years she had remained a voluntary prisoner at Collinwood, ventured as far as the front steps to supervise the hanging of special lanterns above the door. It was a day of unusual happenings.

Of course, Margaret Lucas was left out of the excitement, and Carlos remained on the fringe of things with his usual sneering smile as he watched them prepare for the night of festivity.

Elizabeth, with her usual thoughtfulness, asked Victoria to take a box with a generous sampling of the refreshments prepared for the party over to the invalid. And so that was how Victoria found herself taking tea with the invalid at four o'clock on the afternoon of the party.

"I'm sure you'll be very lovely tonight, my dear." The gray-haired woman smiled behind her heavy dark glasses. "Linda told me you found a rose silk dress in one of the old trunks."

She smiled. "I think it will look nice. The neckline is low, but it's lace edging is so lovely I couldn't bear to change it."

"You must come over tomorrow and show it to me," the invalid said. "I do wish I could attend the party and see everyone."

Victoria felt deep sympathy for her. "Surely you could come and just watch? That shouldn't tax your strength too much."

Margaret Lucas sighed. "I'm afraid not, my dear. I have had a great deal of pain lately. I wouldn't want to chance an attack there. But I will be thinking of you, I promise."

Victoria chatted a little longer, then hurried back to the main house. More than thirty of those invited had written they would come. Burke Devlin had come back from his trip and phoned Victoria he would be there, but he hadn't mentioned anything about the investigation she'd asked him to launch into Professor Veno's past.

This bothered her a little and she intended to question Burke about it when a convenient opportunity presented itself that evening. Since the night the professor had suffered the attack, he had been even stranger in his behavior than usual. Victoria had encountered him at all sorts of odd times wandering about the old mansion and she was curious about what he was up to. She was certain his prowling indicated something.

But then, Collinwood had been a haven of secrets from the beginning of her stay there and she dare not hazard a guess as to what would next be revealed. Ernest also had kept to himself a great deal, but promised her that his concerto was almost completed. Linda had not seen any more of him during this period than had Victoria and as a result had gone about looking pale and resentful even in the face of the approaching party.

Now the great night was at hand. For a time, at least, all gloomy thoughts would be put aside. Victoria paused to gaze into the big living room which had been cleared of furniture and rugs, to offer the great hardwood floor for dancing. A grand piano had been brought from one of the other rooms to serve the orchestra which was to arrive at eight. Garlands of colored ribbon and magic lanterns had been stretched across the ceiling in all directions from the chandelier to the corners of the room. She had never seen the house in such a happy mood.

Suddenly a familiar voice from behind her said, "Hardly the ideal setting for the Phantom Mariner, would you say?"

She wheeled around quickly to face the professor, whose bony, sallow face wore a sneering smile that expressed his disdain for all their preparations.

"I don't think he's expected this evening." she said.

He lifted his eyebrows. "But then, he has a habit of appearing when we least expect him, doesn't he?"

"I'm not worried about tonight."

The professor uttered a small, unpleasant laugh that grated on her nerves. "It is perfectly normal to temporarily forget the unpleasant things in our lives. But they still linger in the background, whether we like it or not."

Victoria couldn't decide what this was supposed to mean, but she was not going to allow herself to be upset on this gala occasion. She said, "If you'll excuse me, I have to hurry and change into my costume."

His burning eyes met hers. "I look forward to seeing you later."

She quickly made her way upstairs to her room, still wondering whether the professor was actually the Phantom Mariner or if the role of the phantom had been played by someone else. It bothered her.

But there was no sign of it on her smiling face when she later descended the stairs to join the others. She was radiantly beautiful in the rose silk and she had done her black hair in a full upsweep to match the fashion of an earlier day. The other women looked equally lovely, and Roger and Ernest were dashing in white tie and tails.

Ernest met her at the foot of the stairs and kissed her hand before a jealous-eyed Linda and all the others. "You look sensationally beautiful," he told her.

For Victoria the affair was a success from the beginning. The orchestra arrived promptly and proved excellent. Elizabeth, Roger and Linda stood at the door to receive the costumed guests as they arrived. Soon the living room floor was filled with dancing couples.

Burke Devlin looked more handsome in his formal attire than Victoria had ever seen him before. He made his way directly to her. "This is quite a night for Collinwood."

"Everyone seems happy about it, if you omit the professor," she told him with a small smile.

Burke frowned and looked around. "Where is he?"

"He hasn't come downstairs since the guests began to arrive," she said. "I doubt if he will show up."

"I see," Burke said. "Has he been bothering you again?"

"Not really. But he has been acting strangely. And he did ask me tonight if I thought the Phantom Mariner would attend the party."

"A jolly thought!" Burke Devlin said grimly. "I'm going to keep an eye out for him. And you take care of yourself."

"I will," she promised. And then she asked the question that had been troubling her. "Did you find out any more about his first wife and daughter?"

"Yes. But I haven't time to go into it here."

She looked up at him earnestly. "Please, I'm so anxious to know the truth."

"You can wait a little. It won't make that much difference."

"But I have waited so long!" she pleaded.

Burke shook his head. "Can't help you at the moment. Eilzabeth has promised me this waltz." And he hurried off to join the mistress of Collinwood and guide her onto the dance floor.

Victoria watched them forlornly, wondering what Burke had discovered. It seemed he was in no hurry to tell her, whatever it was. She was still standing there looking wistful when Ernest came up to her.

"You promised me this waltz," he reminded her, taking her arm.

She smiled faintly. "I'm afraid I'd forgotten."

Ernest took her out onto the floor to join the other costumed couples in the gay, swirling waltz. He nodded toward Burke Devlin and Elizabeth as they began to dance. "I suppose talking to the handsome Burke made you forget everything," he suggested.

Victoria looked amused. "You're not still jealous of Burke?"

"I can't say I liked the solemn way you two were talking. Looked as if there could be something really serious between you."

She laughed as they waltzed close to the orchestra and as they moved away from the music again, she said, "You needn't worry. And while we're on the subject, you didn't help Linda's evening by kissing my hand when I came down the last stair and telling me how pretty I was in front of everyone."

"An earned compliment," Ernest told her. "I have no regrets."

"You must be especially nice to Linda. Be sure to give her plenty of dances. She'll soon be leaving Collinwood and we don't want her going away unhappy."

Ernest studied her as they danced. "You think too much about other people's feelings and not enough about your own. I'll be leaving soon as well. What do you say to that?"

"I'll miss you terribly. I'll be lonely, frightened and sad."

He smiled. "Sounds as if the combination might be formidable enough for me to persuade you to come with me."

She shook her head. "You don't mean that! You don't really want me with you yet, or you'd have discussed it before."

"What makes you so sure?"

She raised an eyebrow. "A woman's intuition, if you need a reason."

"You could be wrong."

"I'm not," she said. The music ended and they applauded. "That was lovely," she said.

Victoria danced with several other guests and then Roger Collins came forward to make her his partner in a lively two-step.

"This is doing me a world of good," he said, puffing slightly from his exertions. "Are you having a pleasant time?"

"It's a wonderful evening," she said.

"I agree," he said as he swung her lightly around. He was a good dancer, in spite of not being in the best condition. "I think it ought to make a change in Elizabeth," he said. "Perhaps it could even lead to her leaving this house once in a while."

"That would be healthy for her," Victoria said. "It is something so touchy I've never spoken to her about it."

Roger nodded. "Nearly twenty years is too long to shut one's self away from the world, no matter how strong the reason may be. It's another of Collinwood's secrets. A thing better forgotten, but you can't make Elizabeth look at it that way."

As they continued dancing to the tuneful music Victoria found herself thinking about Elizabeth and the mystery of her husband who had vanished so suddenly that long time ago. It was typical of the perverse hidden facts that shadowed the old mansion. Even on this night of gaiety all of the guests would be familiar with the story and keeping it in the back of their minds.

The dance ended and Victoria was at once claimed as a partner by Carolyn's boyfriend of the moment, Joe. As she danced, she saw that Ernest and Linda were on the floor together and the girl who so resembled her in looks seemed happy for the first time that evening.

When she left the floor again she consulted with Elizabeth, who suggested they begin bringing out the refreshments within a quarter-hour. With this settled she moved away from the group of which Elizabeth was a part and found herself face to face with Burke Devlin again.

"Are we going to have that talk?" she asked.

He smiled. "If you must. I'll meet you outside by the garden bench. Let us slip out singly so as not to cause any gossip."

She agreed to this at once. Even Ernest had shown jealousy at seeing her in Burke's company. She was eager to hear what he had found out during his brief stay in New York and hurried out the side door to cross the patio and meet him in the garden.

When she stepped out into the darkness she was startled to find how cool it had become. In September the nights in Maine tended to be many degrees lower than the perfect sunny days. With a tiny shiver she headed across the lawn to the bench Burke had mentioned.

As she moved closer to the bench she saw a figure standing there and rushed forward. When she did so the figure revealed itself. She cried out in horror at the sight of the cowled Phantom Mariner and the skull face of death which was the phantom's trade mark.

From behind she heard Burke call her name. "Victoria! Wait!"

As Burke spoke, the dark figure of the Phantom Mariner vanished and she was left alone. She was sobbing in terror as Burke came up to join her.

Placing an arm around her, he asked with alarm, "What's wrong?"

"The ghost! I saw it again!" she said. "It was waiting here!"

Burke looked around in the darkness. "No sign of it now."

"It vanished as soon as you called out," she said.

"Whoever it was must have heard us talking," he said. "Otherwise they wouldn't have been out here waiting for you."

"The professor?" she suggested.

"Probably. He makes a habit of lurking in the shadows."

She pressed close to him, feeling safer in his arms. "Oh, Burke! Even on this night! What is going to happen to me?"

"You're going to protect yourself properly from now on," was his grim rejoinder. He held out something dark and shiny to her. "Take this and use it if you need to."

Even in the darkness she could tell it was a gun. She took it awkwardly and its cold, menacing steel made her tremble. "I've never used any sort of weapon," she said.

"Then it is time you learned how," he told her.

He quickly explained the safety catch and told her to hide it in the pocket of the rose dress. Fortunately there was one large enough to hold it, and it would be well hidden in the voluminous folds of her skirt. She knew he had given her the gun to make her feel more secure, but it really only increased her nervousness. And she was positive she'd never find courage to use it, no matter what the crisis.

With the gun safely away she said, "What have you to tell me?"

"I'll make it quick," Burke said. "We've got to hurry back and I want to watch out for our friend Mark." He paused. "You are wrong."

"Wrong in what?"

"In thinking that the daughter of Mark Collins' first wife might have lived and you could be her. My detective found the death certificates of both baby and mother."

"You're certain," she said, unwilling to admit that she'd come up against another dead end.

"Positive. So you are not Mark's daughter or a Collins. I never thought you were."

"There was a possibility."

"You needn't worry about it any more. But you'd better worry about the professor. I'd say he was on the verge of insanity. There's no telling what he's liable to do."

"I'll remember," she said weakly.

Burke took her arm to guide her back to the house. "Now we'd better join the others."

When she did, it was with a feeling of despair. Everything seemed to be going wrong. She kept an eye open for some sign of the black-garbed professor, but he was nowhere in sight among the happy party group. Then Elizabeth reminded her that it was time to begin serving the refreshments. She was glad to have this diversion to keep her busy. It left her no time to think.

Not until the final dance did she find herself in Ernest's arms again and he at once sensed the change in her mood. With a worried expression, he asked, "What's wrong? You don't seem like the same person I started the evening with."

She attempted a smile. "Perhaps I'm weary."

He eyed her sharply. "You're sure it's nothing more than that?"

"I'm all right," she told him.

"I hope so," he said, but she could tell he was not convinced.

The dance ended and after a short period of conversation the guests left. It was a quarter to two before Elizabeth closed the door on the final couple and turned to them with a tired smile.

"It was a success, wasn't it?" she said.

Roger was jubilant. "Just like old times!"

"It was wonderful, Mother!" Carolyn exulted.

Linda gave Ernest a wistful glance and told Elizabeth, "I'm sure you did everything possible to make the party a happy one."

"What do you say, Victoria?" Elizabeth asked with a smile especially for her.

"It's a night I'll always remember," she said truthfully.

"And so will I," Elizabeth agreed. "Now it's time we all went up and had ourselves some sleep."

Ernest saw Victoria to her door, and after again complimenting her on her appearance, kissed her goodnight and went on to his own room. Victoria unlocked her door and switched on the light. She was about to start removing her dress when there was a light knock on her door.

With a slight frown on her pretty face, Victoria hesitated a moment. Then, realizing the others were still all awake and the danger was minimal, she went over and opened the door. It was Linda, looking girlishly forlorn.

"I'm sorry to disturb you," the lovely dark girl said, "but I can't get these hooks undone at the back of my dress. Would you mind helping me?"

"Of course not," Victoria said, relieved. "We may as well go back to your room and then you can slip the dress right off."

"Thank you," Linda said gratefully. "I didn't think the hooks would give me so much trouble."

She followed Linda into her room and then unhooked the dress for her and waited until she had taken it off. Linda in long white petticoat and bra saw her to the door and they said goodnight again.

Victoria started back down the corridor to her own room. They hadn't discussed the party in their short time together, which she felt was just as well, since she knew Linda had not had as good a time as she'd hoped. Ernest had once again made it clear who he preferred.

When she reached her own door she saw the light in her room was turned off. She tried to remember whether she had left it off or on and couldn't be certain about it. With a sigh she stepped inside and was about to reach for the light switch when she felt something slip down over her head and tighten around her neck.

She gasped and tried to call out, but the thing that circled her neck was continually drawn more taut and was quickly cutting off her breathing. She was being dragged back in the darkness. She clawed out wildly, desperately. There were hands holding the end of the cord around her throat; and she found them and struggled until she had momentarily freed herself. Then she groped in her pocket for the gun and fired blindly in the direction of her assailant. She heard a sharp moan and the sound of a body slumping to the floor.

For a long moment she stood there with the gun in her hand, sobbing with fear and unable to make a move. Then she heard running footsteps and voices coming toward her room. The sound of the shot had roused the household. The light was switched on and she saw them all crowding in the doorway. Roger was the first to enter the room.

"What?" He stopped as he saw the body on the floor.

Victoria was staring hard at it also. Stretched out there was the familiar figure of the Phantom Mariner. The long black garb and the cowl framed the grinning skeleton face. A growing pool of blood on the floor oozed from the wound made by the bullet. She saw that the skeleton face was merely a cheap rubber mask.

And Roger also was aware of this at the same instant. For with a quick glance in Victoria's direction first he knelt down by the bleeding figure and fumbled to remove the mask.

When it came away Victoria gasped. For she was staring down at the face of Margaret Lucas.

A Margaret Lucas without dark glasses or the iron-gray wig!

A Margaret Lucas of striking middle-aged beauty!

Victoria rushed forward to her. "Mrs. Lucas!" She bent by the figure.

There was a flicker of movement in the pale, lovely face and the great sad brown eyes of Margaret Lucas opened and fixed on Victoria. "Not Margaret Lucas," she said in a low voice. "Wife of Mark Collins! My daughter!" And she began to cough weakly.

Linda, who had been standing with the others, now came forward to kneel with Roger and Victoria. "Mother!" she exclaimed. "I should have recognized you. But I had never seen more than a snapshot and with the glasses and gray hair –"

She didn't finish, for the injured woman had stopped coughing and opened her eyes again. She gazed up at Linda lovingly. "Did it for you," she said.

"Oh, Mother!" Linda's voice was anguished.

"Too long apart," her mother said in a faint voice. "His fault! Wanted you to myself again. Had to kill him and see you married to Ernest. Had to kill Victoria too, because she stood in the way."

"It doesn't matter," Linda said, bending close and touching her lips to her mother's cheek. "It's over now and it will be all right."

The woman shook her head. "No good. I failed. Mark wins again. Don't hate me for it."

She let her gaze wander to Victoria. "Nor you! I . . . " Her voice faded and she suddenly went limp.

Professor Veno spoke coldly from the doorway. "I have phoned Ellsworth for the ambulance."

Linda was weeping over the body of her dead mother and Victoria's arm was around her.

So it was Roger who rose to face the grim, black-garbed Professor.

Roger said, "No need for an ambulance. She's dead."

The professor shrugged, an expression of indifference on the sallow face. "In that case, it's a matter for the police."

Roger asked, "Don't you feel any sorrow at all?"

"Why should I?" Professor Veno asked scornfully. "She brought about her own death by this ridiculous masquerade."

Victoria paid no more attention to what was said. Nor did she try to keep a distinct record of the events of the hours that followed. The body was taken from her room. The police came and asked questions.

She was lying in bed in the late morning when Ernest came to the door with a tray of coffee and toast. He placed it on her bedside table and sat down with her.

"It's all looked after as far as the police are concerned," he said. "There will be an inquest, but it will be strictly a matter of routine. No blame is attached to you. You did what you did in self defense."

She hid her face in her hands for a moment. "Linda. How is she?"

"She has plenty of courage," Ernest said. "She's taking it in her stride. She knows where the true blame lies—with her father."

Dropping her hands, Victoria stared at the young violinist in despair. "What will happen now?"

"What should have happened long ago," he said grimly. "She's planning to return to New York on her own and find herself some kind of career. Money is no problem and she no longer feels obligated to stay with the professor."

"It will be better for her," Victoria agreed.

"Of course it will," he said bitterly. "She should have done it long ago. Then maybe this wouldn't have happened."

"Where did Carlos fit into it?"

Ernest sighed. "The police questioned him. He's in a nasty spot. It seems he knew that Margaret was trying to kill you from the beginning. But he wouldn't betray her. All he was willing to do was warn you."

"He tried to do that several times," she admitted. "Carlos was very devoted to Linda's mother. He knew she was suffering from an incurable disease that was predicted to cause her death in a few months. He claims he thought she would become too ill to continue her attempts against your life. I don't think the police will be too hard on him."

"I hope not," she said.

Ernest passed her the cup of coffee. "Try some of this," he said. "You can't have had any sleep at all."

"I've not really closed my eyes."

"You'll have to relax and rest now," he said. "The nightmare is over."

Roger had the village doctor call on her later in the morning and give her a sedative. And by the time she awoke Professor Veno had left the house to take lodgings at the Collinsport Hotel where he would stay until after the inquest.

When she went downstairs for the first time after the awful events it was Linda she saw first. The girl came forward to meet her. "Are you better?"

"Yes," Victoria said. Tears welled in her eyes. "Can you forgive me?"

"There is nothing to forgive," Linda assured her. With a sad smile she added, "Unless it is your allowing Ernest to fall in love with you."

The inquest was held promptly. And when it was over Professor Veno left Collinsport for what most people believed would be the last time. He left few behind who wished to ever see him again. Linda ignored him completely when he tried to approach her at the finish of the inquest.

Linda left Collinwood a few days later to go to New York and find an apartment and the beginning of a new life. Carlos Marelli was given a stern reprimand by the coroner, but was allowed his freedom. He listened with his usual sneering attitude and also departed from the village at once.

So now there was only Ernest remaining. And on a foggy Monday in the first week of October he said goodbye. Victoria went out to the taxi with him and he took her in his arms for a final kiss.

"Write soon and often," she said.

"I will," he promised with a sad smile. "I'll let you know how the concerto is received."

"It's bound to be a success. I'm sure of it!" Victoria said.

"I'm dedicating it to you," he told her.

She was overwhelmed. "How can you?" she asked. "A girl without a real name."

"There isn't anyone who truly knows you who feels your name is of the slightest importance," he said. "Anyhow, I like it. Victoria Winters!" And he touched his lips lightly to hers in parting.

Victoria stood waving after the taxi as it vanished in the fog. Then she turned and walked slowly back to the house. Another parting! There had been too many of them. How long would it be until she and Ernest would share the future together? Or would it ever happen?

Elizabeth was waiting for her just inside the front door. She offered her a sympathetic glance. "I know," she said. "You're feeling blue."

Victoria nodded. "I've nothing to look forward to, now that he's gone."

"Nonsense," the older woman said, placing an arm around her. "You'll hear from him. And he'll come back. You must know that. There are many chapters of our lives at Collinwood still to be lived. Surely now they will be happy ones."

Victoria smiled at the mysterious woman who had become her friend as well as her employer. Slowly a warm feeling of confidence returned to her.

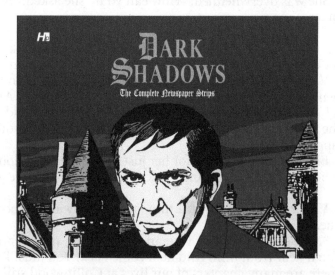